Interview for Death . . .

It had been a long morning. I had read to Mrs. Dobb from Miss Charlotte Brontë's strangely disturbing romance, *Jane Eyre*. We had talked of many things. But I was still startled when she asked, suddenly, "What do you want from me?"

I suspected that the nature of our relationship would depend on my answer. "I'm not sure I want anything from you," I said. "I'm not even sure I should accept the job."

Mrs. Dobb looked at me with one of the elaborate expressions I was to become so familiar with. This one combined disappointment, disapproval, and challenge. "I suppose you want as much of my money as you can get. But I'd be disappointed if that were all you wanted."

I found myself speaking against my will: "What if I said I wanted your life?"

We both smiled. Mrs. Dobb relaxed, and her eyes closed before her smile faded. I sat and watched her fall asleep. She looked beautiful, vulnerable, and happy.

I knew I could not resist becoming her companion, although I thought I might regret my decision someday . . .

Ken Greenhall

POCKET BOOKS

New York   London   Toronto   Sydney   Tokyo

Another *Original* publication of POCKET BOOKS

POCKET BOOKS, a division of Simon & Schuster Inc.
1230 Avenue of the Americas, New York, N.Y. 10020

ISBN 978-1-9821-3010-7

First Pocket Books printing August 1988

10 9 8 7 6 5 4 3 2 1

POCKET and colophon are trademarks of
Simon & Schuster Inc.

Printed in the U.S.A.

1 | *Who I Am and How I Live*

Someone—a neighbor or even a well-groomed person on a television news program—may have told you lies about me and my father. They want you to believe that we are deranged or even inhuman, but I assure you that neither of those things is true. I hope you let me tell you the truth, for I'm sure you were brought up, as I was, to believe that truth creates understanding.

If you live in a certain kind of American town, it is possible that you once saw us. You might have passed us occasionally as we strolled along a side street in the early evening. You would have nodded and smiled at us, but you would have been uneasy, sensing that our failings were unlike your own. You would have been relieved when, after a few weeks or months, you saw our expressionless faces gazing at you through the window of a departing interstate bus. And later, when you had almost forgotten us, a revelation on the local television news might have confirmed your suspicions about us and made you congratulate yourself on your ability to recognize evil. But you knew the news story was incomplete. You wanted to know the whole truth, even though you knew it would be unsettling.

Let me tell you.

My name is Jillian Cole, and as you might expect of someone in my profession, I have always been well liked. I am thirty-four years old, have an easy smile and ample breasts, and always listen carefully when someone speaks to me.

My life at present is not conventional, but unless you are the kind of person who is given to dark sentimentality, you would find me ordinary. If you had to classify my former life, however, the term *ordinary* would probably not occur to you.

I was what in more romantic times was called a gentlewoman's companion. I was a person who knew the curious stimulation of sitting at a strange bedside in the darkness and holding a hand deformed by age—a hand no one else wanted to hold. My employer was aware that when I took her hand it was not a professional act but the personal gesture of someone who understood and respected death. She willingly entrusted to me not just her hand but her possessions and her life.

The time I was allowed away from my employer I spent with Father, who said that a professional companion was merely a genteel prostitute. I didn't mind his accusation. "Like father, like daughter," I said.

He smiled. "I wasn't genteel," he said.

But he knew that there were many people—women in particular—who would have described him as a saint and martyr; women on whose brow or breasts his hands once rested; women who said his touch healed them and who would be resentful and envious to learn that I had become the only one he touched.

I was closest to happiness when I was with Father in his furnished room, sipping whiskey and listening to stories about his life. Occasionally, I would guide his hand to my face so his fingers could gently trace the imperfect curve of my nose.

Now that he was sightless, he was more attractive than ever, his thick white hair contrasting dramatically with the darkness of his glasses. His less-than-intelligent eyes were his only flawed feature, and now that his weakness was concealed behind opaque glass, there was nothing to detract from his handsomeness.

Father said he was atoning—atoning not for what he had done voluntarily but for what he had been led to do by the people who talked of God and sex.

I didn't believe in atonement.

And I wondered if Father would have expected me to believe if he had been with me on those remarkable nights; if he had heard the gasps that preceded the absolute silence; if he knew that I had not only been an observer of death but had also been its helper.

In our travels, Father and I sought out a certain type of town. It had to have a human scale of sounds: neither the harsh traffic of the city nor the unnatural silence of the suburbs. On summer evenings we wanted to hear the voices of neighbors on screened porches—voices muffled by the heavy foliage of the tree-lined streets.

We wanted to be among people who, if they noticed us, would be too polite to question us.

We would reach the town in the middle of the day. The bus driver, with his reassuring array of safety badges and his military officer's cap, would retrieve our scuffed but expensive baggage from the storage compartment, hesitating slightly when he reached the long case containing Father's electronic keyboard.

Then, as Father and I stood in the center of the town with our carefully selected belongings, we would begin our deception. I looked for a tavern. I knew precisely what kind of place to look for. It should never be on the main street and should never be newly decorated and call itself a pub. It should be in the middle of a block, and its unwashed windows should contain three or four neon advertising signs whose flickering, buzzing tubes spelled out the names of beers. If the town was laid out in the standard railroad plan, with the east–west streets named for trees and the north–

south streets numbered, the bar would be on a numbered street. If the bar was named for a woman and was on Seventh Street, I was most pleased. It would, of course, be on the wrong side of the tracks.

I would settle Father in a booth with a glass of bourbon and would go to the public phone to begin covering our tracks. I regretted that it was necessary to be evasive and deceptive in our travels, but I was sure there were always people who would like to follow us and punish us for acts they imperfectly understood.

The tavern's ambience—the indistinguishable smells of stale beer and urine, the sexual scribblings surrounding the wall phone—encouraged deceit.

I placed a call to another town, a town the bus had stopped at a half-hour earlier, where I had left the bus and found a telephone number for the local taxi service.

In this case, the town I called was Serena, Iowa. My call was answered by a young woman. I told her we had missed our stop on the bus and that we wanted her to drive us back to Serena. She agreed to pick us up outside the bar—Elaine's.

I returned to Father, who had ordered a second drink and was listening to a young woman who sat at the bar but had turned to face him. Strangers like to talk to Father, and I'm not certain why they do. Perhaps they feel less threatened by someone who can't see them, or perhaps their conversation is an act of sympathy.

The young woman spoke with an energy that seemed real but was out of place. "You know the joke," she said, "about the town that was so small the local prostitute was a virgin?"

Father grinned.

The woman continued. "Well, it's not that bad here in Plaines, but almost. Where I want to be is in a building with more than three stories; Chicago along the lake or New York by Central Park. I see all the movies about call girls. *Klute.* I loved *Klute.* In the movies, they try to kill the girls, but I don't think they do in real life."

"There isn't any real life," Father said. "That's what the Chinese believe—that we. aren't really alive."

The woman at the bar laughed. "I never knew that. But how *would* I know? We don't even have a Chinese restaurant here."

She was charmed by Father. It was time for me to stop the conversation before he said something that would make her want to follow us.

I didn't have to say anything to the woman. She turned away as soon as I sat down across from Father.

And I didn't have to say anything to Father to let him know I was back.

"Spoilsport," he said.

"Lecher," I said.

"What does she look like?"

I glanced into the mirror behind the bar and met the eyes of the woman. She had been staring at me but immediately looked down at the bar. Perhaps she felt, as I did, that there was danger in reflected images.

I said to Father, "She's unexpectedly plain, considering her occupation or hobby or whatever it is."

"The virtuous look. Some men are excited by it." Father paused, and I knew he was about to deliver one of his aphorisms. Then he said, "You know you're in a town that takes its religion seriously if the hookers don't wear makeup."

I could never be sure if his words of wisdom were improvised or whether he had picked them up in his days among the evangelists.

"It's not a time for chatting," I said, remembering the need for discretion. For the next half-hour I was silent, and Father made only the occasional hummings and grunts that he makes when he is thinking about music. Four or five people drifted in and out of the bar, glancing at us with a fascination they tried to conceal. The young woman's forced animation faded a little more with each beer she drank, and she began to stare openly at us.

"We're attracting attention," I said.

"Everyone attracts attention in small-town bars. There's a lot of unused attention. The customers are always looking for a show; they're hoping we'll do something they can go home and tell the family about."

Although I was sure he wasn't doing it intentionally, Father was stirring up some of the feelings of guilt I felt toward him. He had grown up in a big city— Detroit—and despite his blindness, he had an intense interest in the things around him. Small towns restricted him, and if it hadn't been for his music, he would have found our way of life intolerable.

"I know you miss the city, Father. Maybe we should get back on a bus and head for Chicago. I could set you up there."

"You wouldn't stay with me, though?"

"I could visit you between jobs."

"No, no. I like to be near you. And big cities are for sinning. I've done more than my share of that. I need some small-town repenting."

We had both spent enough time in small towns to know that the darker forms of behavior achieved some of their most exotic expressions in such places. That is why I practiced my vocation away from cities.

Father and I seldom spoke of my vocation, but as I have said, he was never unaware of what went on around him.

He also understood that each person has individual needs, and he knew that I was not a woman who did things for frivolous reasons. He trusted me with a completeness that can only grow out of love. But I knew that the strongest affections can fade. "You'll want to leave me someday. You mustn't hesitate to tell me when that happens."

"If it does happen, it'll probably be because you exposed me to bad music." The reference was to an old jukebox, all curves and glowing colors, which had been brought to life and was playing a sentimental, overproduced country-and-western ballad.

"A good guitar player at the mercy of a bad singer and fifty studio hacks," Father said.

He had been known to make offensive remarks to innocent bystanders when he was being subjected to music he didn't like, and it seemed wiser for us to wait outside. The day had been overcast, and now that the sun had almost set, we wouldn't be too conspicuous standing on the street. I moved our luggage out to the curb, and five minutes later our driver arrived in a battered station wagon, and we were on our way to Serena.

I began to relax. The station wagon was warm and smelled of earth. We were passing through a prosperous agricultural area. Most of the widely scattered homes of the farmers were large, new, and suburban-styled. Next to each house, like a large mushroom from another planet, sat a dish antenna.

Once more our reflections were being watched. Because the road was straight and smooth and there was little traffic, the driver was able to give most of her attention to us through the rearview mirror. For the second time that afternoon, I exchanged glances with someone in a mirror. It was an intimate act, like looking into one's own eyes.

The driver took my glance as a signal that it was all right to talk to us.

"Do you have relatives in Serena?" she asked.

"No. We just thought it was pretty—like its name."

"Then you'll need a place to stay."

I smiled. "Yes. And a job to keep me out of mischief."

"What kind of job?"

"I'm a companion—for old people."

The driver's eyes showed confusion. "I'm not sure we use those around here. We use family. And there's a church-run home."

"Well, if you should hear of anything, I'd appreciate your letting me know." And then it was necessary for me to tell a lie. "There's one more thing," I said. "My husband may come looking for me. I've just left him. If he should come to you and ask if you've seen me, I'd appreciate it if you could say no. Not that I'm asking you to lie, but maybe you could just say you don't give information about your customers."

The driver was silent. I glanced at the rearview mirror. She was looking at me skeptically. I held her eyes and said, "I wouldn't ask you except that he likes to hurt me."

"Beats you, you mean?"

I nodded. The driver looked away. I thought maybe the subject of violent and abusive men was something she understood. "Well, in that case," she said.

"Thank you. I knew I would be safe in Serena." I was beginning to believe that was true. We rode on toward our refuge in silence. In the near-darkness, the cornfields, with their silhouetted remnants of the harvest, looked like neglected graveyards.

2 | *Meeting Mrs. Dobb*

"Another home, dear," I said to Father.

I led him through his new room, unpacking his clothes: the white shirts and underwear; the black socks, trousers, jackets, and shoes. I placed them all in the usual locations—an arrangement so orderly that it went beyond the visible.

Father wandered the room, counting paces from bed to dresser, dresser to table, table to bathroom; counting and memorizing; touching surfaces scarred by other people in their tantrums and blunders.

"It smells clean," he said.

"It *is* clean."

"The last one here before me was a woman."

I wasn't sure how he knew that, but I could tell it pleased him.

The town of Serena had drawn Father and me into its life without hesitation, as though it had been waiting for us.

The taxi driver had taken us to a rooming house run by a widow with the improbable name of Mrs. Tickle. Unlike her name, she showed no signs of frivolity. Obviously, decades of boarders had left her with few illusions. But father overwhelmed Mrs. Tickle. She was trembling with sympathy and attraction and couldn't stop smiling. I paid her a month's rent in advance and asked if she knew of an elderly woman who might want me as a companion.

13

"Definitely," she said. "Mrs. Dobb. I'll call her for you in the morning."

I wondered whether Mrs. Tickle would have been so eager to help me if it hadn't been a way of getting me away from Father.

The next morning, I spoke to Mrs. Dobb, who asked me to come over immediately.

Her house, which was large and richly decorated with jigsaw scrollwork, had an unsettling lack of symmetry. It was a two-story structure in two sections, but one section was significantly wider and higher than the other. In the center of the house there would have to be oddly shaped corridors with occasional three- or four-step rises. I supposed I might eventually grow fond of the house's eccentricities, but my first impression was uneasiness. I was more attracted to the huge trees (sycamores, I thought) that surrounded the house like sentinels. In the summer, the house would hardly be visible.

A housekeeper, who looked at me without either interest or resentment, led me up a curved staircase to a second-floor bedroom. She knocked, opened the door, and left.

I entered Mrs. Dobb's bedroom. The dim light and badly placed furniture reminded me of Father's room. But there was a difference: This was the room not of someone who couldn't see but of someone who did not want to see—or perhaps did not want to *be* seen. The furnishings were old and poorly matched, intended not to please the eye but to serve as an index to the past. The room was dominated by an enormous bed canopied in dusty bronze-colored brocade.

"I'm Jillian Cole," I said.

Mrs. Dobb was barely visible in the shadows, a small, pale specter propped up against the dark headboard of the bed.

"Stand near the window," she said. Her voice was like something called forth in a séance.

I went to the window and drew aside a velvet drape—a faded maroon fabric that clashed with the material of the bed's canopy. Dust glittered in a beam of autumn sunlight. I turned to face the old woman. Her expression was challenging but not displeased.

"I was expecting a black person," she said. "You're not a black person, are you?"

"No. But I'm the next best thing."

Mrs. Dobb's skeptical squint changed to a wide-eyed, cautious gaze. We looked at each other in silence for a few moments. I wondered what a companionship between us might be like or whether it was even a possibility.

Mrs. Dobb said, "You've been a companion to other women, I assume?"

"Yes. Six."

"I'm the seventh. A magical number."

"I don't believe in magic," I said.

"Of course you do. What about the magic of love? You've experienced that, haven't you?"

"I suppose I experienced love with my ex-husband, but it seemed more like insanity than magic."

"And there are no men in your life now?"

If I hadn't spent so much time with old and lonely women in recent years, I might have wondered whether Mrs. Dobb had some lesbian inclinations. But I assumed she was simply inquisitive about my emotions, or that she wanted to know if there was someone she would have to share my attention with.

I said, "My father travels with me."

"He's here in Serena?"

"Yes. In a rooming house. But he's self-sufficient. He won't take much of my time."

"Perhaps your father believes in magic."

"Not exactly. You could say that magic believes in *him*. If you consider faith healing a type of magic."

"Is that his profession?"

"It was for a time. He never believed in it, but he couldn't escape it."

"Our talents can be burdensome. The fortunate people are those who have modest talents."

"Like a talent for companionship?"

"Certainly. But I am among the truly fortunate, those whose talents are nonexistent."

I didn't believe Mrs. Dobb had no talents. I was sure she had them and that they were distinctive. We were staring at each other with excited curiosity. There were pitfalls in this kind of talk. It would be better, I thought, to let my interviewer lead the conversation.

Mrs. Dobb continued. "I don't require talents in my companion, but I do require certain other traits. She should have strong emotions but should seldom, if ever, display them. She should be articulate but ill educated."

Mrs. Dobb wanted to trade surprises. I offered her the least surprising response: silence.

"Do you have those traits, my dear?"

"I have three of them," I said. Actually, I had them all. I wanted her to wonder—or to ask—which one I lacked.

She didn't ask. Instead she said, "Three would have been my guess."

I smiled. The tension in Mrs. Dobb's expression vanished for a moment but then returned as she prepared to speak. I wondered if speaking caused her pain.

"What are your views on death?" she asked.

I felt the muscles in my temples tighten, and I made an effort to look mildly surprised rather than frightened. Why did she bring up the subject of death? Did she distrust me already? Had she guessed my secret? Was my concern with death becoming obvious? I began to think I should look elsewhere for employment. Mrs. Dobb's mind was too active and unpredictable.

She spoke again. "You're not too young to have opinions about death. Perhaps you're timid."

I smiled. "No," I said. "Death should be valued and respected."

"Should it be sought?"

"It's not necessary to seek death," I said. "It's just necessary to be patient."

Mrs. Dobb seemed disappointed with my answer. "To be patient with death," she said, "is merely to be a good loser. I've been too patient for too long. I feel the need to be in control now. You can understand that, can't you?"

"Yes."

"I thought so. Control is what companionship is about, I believe. The companion wants either to control someone or to be controlled."

"Is it that simple?"

"Yes. All things are simpler than people make them out to be. Things can be subtle, but they're simple. That's what good psychotherapists know. They look for the simple truth."

"I don't believe in psychotherapy."

"I'm not concerned with your beliefs, my dear. I'm concerned with whether you want to control or to be controlled."

"It needn't be that way. I could show you another way."

"That sounds like religious talk to me. Are you religious?"

"No. I'm an Episcopalian."

"That's a relief. Good works and gentility. There's no danger there . . . but there's probably boredom. Will you be boring, Jillian?"

"I'll be what you want me to be."

In apparent excitement, Mrs. Dobb put the heels of

her hands on the bed's satin spread and tried to push herself higher against the headboard, but her hands slipped. She looked at me with what could have been either embarrassment or anger. "Aren't you going to help me sit up?" she asked.

"I didn't want to seem controlling," I said. I went and placed my hands under her armpits. She responded by placing her hands on my forearms. Her body had an unexpected strength—a firmness in her grip, in the muscles of her upper torso, and even in her breasts, which pressed against my wrists. She was strong enough to have sat up without my help. I realized she had just wanted me to be close to her.

Then she put her mouth against my ear. "I think you're the one I've been waiting for," she whispered.

I backed away. Did I dare work for this woman? It would be a challenge, but a dangerous one. I looked for a way out. "I'm afraid I don't have any references," I said.

Mrs. Dobb acknowledged my announcement with a glance, but she didn't reply to it. Instead she said, "Come sit next to me." I looked around for a chair. The room was almost a mausoleum, I thought. The furniture wasn't meant to be moved. I took a chair from against a wall and dragged it to Mrs. Dobb's bedside. The chair, which was straight-backed and uncomfortable, was made of black wood carved in a pattern of abstract curves that made me think of breasts and thighs. It was remarkably heavy.

I sat next to Mrs. Dobb and looked carefully at the room. Its true size was concealed by the deep shadows, the plum-and-gold wallpaper, and the massiveness of the bed. Mrs. Dobb was looking at me with apparent pleasure. "This room is an appropriate setting for you," she said.

"Dark solidity, you mean?"

"I like those qualities."

"You prefer them to beauty?"

"You don't consider yourself beautiful?" Mrs. Dobb said. She peered at me. "No. You're attractive but not beautiful. That's fortunate, of course."

"Is beauty a misfortune?"

"Yes. We nonbeauties tend to victimize the beauties. We want revenge."

Mrs. Dobb seemed too interested in topics such as control and revenge. She was alone too much, I thought, and she clearly needed a companion. But I still wasn't sure I was the one she needed.

Mrs. Dobb closed her eyes and held out her hand to me. The hand was like a desert plant. It was loosely closed and was turned palm down, the prominent veins standing out like exposed roots. She turned her palm upward and extended her fingers slowly, like dry, pale petals.

I knew that if I took her hand, I would be sealing a bargain—a bargain whose terms I didn't understand. Gradually, as if beyond my control, my own hand moved out and came to rest in hers, which immediately tightened in a grip that confirmed the strength I had already sensed in her body. Her eyes were open now, but she still was not looking at me. She began to breathe heavily, as if exhausted by the exertion of gripping my hand. Her expression combined pleasure and discomfort. She looked like someone who was watching a movie in which a villain dies deservedly but horribly.

Gradually, Mrs. Dobb's grip relaxed, and her eyes closed again. "You have a pleasant voice," she said. "Do you enjoy reading aloud? I will expect you to read to me whether you enjoy it or not."

"I'm not dramatic," I said. "I use the same voice for everything."

"But do you enjoy it?"

"Reading fiction aloud makes me uneasy. It's as if I'm breaking confidences."

"Bring a book," Mrs. Dobb said. She took her hand from mine and pointed to a corner of the room, where there was a glass-doored cabinet containing a haphazard collection of books with bindings ranging from paper to leather. They were all well worn. I went to the case and took a book at random. It was Charlotte Brontë's *Jane Eyre*—an old leather-bound edition with small, hard-to-read type. I took it to the window and opened it at a page marked by a thin red ribbon. I read aloud a passage in which Jane is talking to her employer, Mr. Rochester. I read slowly and with pleasure. The governess and her employer spoke formally and aggressively to each other, but there was a passionate attraction behind their words. Then I reached an exchange that made me pause. Mr. Rochester spoke first:

"You are human and fallible."

"I am; so are you—what then?"

"The human and fallible should not arrogate a power with which the divine and perfect alone can be safely entrusted."

"What power?"

"That of saying of any strange, unsanctioned line of action, 'Let it be right.'"

Was I, I wondered, a person who had taken a strange, unsanctioned line of action in my life? Had Mrs. Dobb sensed that, and had she somehow forced me to choose this book to read?

She said, "Has something disturbed you, my dear? That's one of Miss Brontë's purposes, don't you think . . . romantic disturbance? Some of us like that more than others, of course."

I didn't know what she was implying. I began to read again, and at one point Mrs. Dobb spoke a line of

Mr. Rochester's with me: "You are afraid of me, because I talk like a sphinx?"

I read alone: "Your language is enigmatical, sir; but though I am bewildered, I am certainly not afraid."

I closed the book, and we smiled at each other.

"How did you make me choose this book?" I asked.

"You chose it, Jillian. Just as you chose Serena and me."

"But you may not want to choose *me*. As I said, I have no references."

"That's not important to me; although it will be important to my son, David. He will also most likely find it important to ask you to grant him a sexual encounter. I imagine you, like most people, will find the request ridiculous and unconvincing."

"Does your son live here with you?"

"No. But he lives near enough to visit whenever he needs anything—which is frequently. David never has as much money as he would like to have, and he believes my only remaining function is to supply him with cash. He is mistaken about that, as he is about almost everything else."

Mrs. Dobb lowered her eyes and was silent for a minute. When she looked up again, she seemed startled to see me. "David is a twin," she said, and was silent again. But this time she continued to peer at me intently through her cataract-gray eyes.

"The idea of twins has always been disturbing to me," I said.

"It has always seemed grotesque to me. I was depressed for months after my twins were born. They behaved normally during their childhood—there were even periods of affection—but I sensed a capacity for the extraordinary in them. I was right—or at least half right. They pass for ordinary, but that isn't really enough, is it?"

"Maybe that's all you can expect. Maybe you're being unfair to your children."

"Perhaps. I don't concern myself with fairness—as you'll find out when you become my companion."

"You're offering me the job?"

"My son will do that. He will have a contract drawn up."

"Even without references?"

"I told you I don't want your references. What I want is your devotion—your soul, if you should happen to have one. *Do* you have one?"

"I thought so once."

"When you were about thirteen, I imagine."

"Yes. About then."

"That was glands. But you may have a soul in any case. If you have one, I'll find it."

We smiled aggressively at each other—the kind of smiles that often signal the end of a conversation. But I sensed that Mrs. Dobb had something else to say. I went to the window and drew the drapes closed. In the dimmer light, she seemed to regain some strength. I sat down and waited.

Eventually she spoke. "I've told you what I want from you. What do you want from me?"

I wasn't prepared for the question, and I suspected that the nature of our relationship would depend on my answer. "I'm not sure that I want anything from you," I said. "I'm not even sure I should accept the job."

Mrs. Dobb looked at me with one of the elaborate expressions I was to become so familiar with. This one combined disappointment, disapproval, and challenge. "You're not afraid of me, are you? I know that most people tend to find me formidable, but I was beginning to think that in this instance I am the one who should be apprehensive. In any case, I'm not a threat to you, my dear. I'm an opportunity."

I hesitated.

"You must want something from me; otherwise you

wouldn't be here. I suppose you want as much of my money as you can get. But I'd be disappointed if that were all you wanted. That would put you on a level with my son."

I found myself speaking against my will. "What if I said I wanted your life?"

"I'd be flattered. No one else wants it. *I* certainly don't. And perhaps it would be a fair trade. Your soul for my life."

We both smiled again. Mrs. Dobb relaxed, and her eyes closed before her smile faded.

I sat and watched her fall asleep. She looked beautiful, vulnerable, and happy.

I knew I could not resist becoming her companion, although I thought I might regret my decision someday.

3 | *An Evening with Father*

I had knocked on Father's door before I entered, but I wasn't sure he had heard me. He looked like a hypnotized insect. Massive black headphones were clamped over his ears, and he was crouched over his electric keyboard, which rested on a low coffee table. The keyboard was what made his life tolerable now, he claimed, and he spent most of his waking time improvising for himself—his inventions flowing from his fingertips to the keyboard and back to his ears through the headphones. The keyboard was the only machine he admired, the only exception he made to his central belief that machines are the feces of the mind.

Just as I was about to speak to him, he said, "I'll be through in a minute."

I stood and watched him. I was moved, as always, by his odd intensity. He stood up suddenly and removed his headset. He reached out to a nearby lamp and put his hand against the shade to feel the heat that would tell him it was turned on.

"That's an unattractive lamp," I said.

"It's sturdy and plain," he said. "That's the way I like my lamps—and my women, for that matter." He held out his arms, and I placed my sturdiness and plainness in his embrace. "Let's go out on the town," he said.

"It's too early. And there is no town to go out on."

"There's always somewhere. Always. A lounge, a

piano bar, a club, a saloon, or, best of all, a roadhouse. And there's always a piano player who knows about Bud Powell and Tadd Dameron and who needs a sympathetic listener."

"Not always. You're thinking of Detroit in the 1950s."

"I do tend to think about that, don't I?"

I led Father to a comfortable old sofa. We sat down side by side. "I'll make some coffee," I said.

"Coffee?" Father was disappointed that I hadn't suggested having something alcoholic.

"You like coffee."

"It's second best."

"That's what I said to Mrs. Dobb. She asked me if I was black, and I said I was the next best thing."

"You could have been black. I half expected it; your mother was full of surprises in those days."

Father lapsed into silence. I supposed he was thinking about the night I was born. It was a snowy night in 1951, and it was the most important night of his life. But, as he has often told me, it was important not because of my birth but because he went from the hospital to a club named the El Sino and for the first time heard Charlie Parker perform in person.

It was time for me to bring Father into the present. I didn't mind hearing his reminiscences, but unless I distracted him from his memories occasionally, he tended to lose his sense of reality. (He pretends to believe reality is overrated, anyway.) Also, I preferred his evangelical stories to his jazz stories. As far as I can tell, the most interesting thing about jazz musicians is their music. They usually spend so much of their time playing their instruments that they don't have time to do or to learn anything else.

I got up to make the coffee in the dented drip pot we traveled with. "We should talk about the present," I said. "About our new friends. Mrs. Tickle, for example. She seems fond of you."

"What does she look like?"

"Maternal, not displeased with life, handsome. She probably wears foundation garments during all waking hours."

"I approve. What about *your* new friend?"

"Mrs. Dobb? She's *not* maternal, indifferent to life, or handsome. She probably thinks foundation garments are dishonest and has never worn them."

"Is she healthy?"

"I haven't found out yet. But she's tough."

"Then we're likely to stay put in Serena for a while?"

"I hope so. I know you'd like to settle down somewhere for a change."

"No I wouldn't. I've always been on the road one way or another."

"But traveling is less appealing when you get older."

"If you're not careful, everything is less appealing. But I'm careful. I don't like as many things, but the things I do like, I like more."

The coffee was ready. We always made it double strength and drank it black. I put a half-full mug into Father's hands. He took a sip. "I like coffee more," he said. "I first realized I was getting old when the only two substances I was abusing were bourbon and coffee. No smoking or snorting; no uppers or downers. The secret of old age—tell this to Mrs. Dobb—is not being less excited about more things, but being more excited about less things."

"I'm not sure Mrs. Dobb gets excited about anything."

"Maybe that's why she hired you—to help her get excited about something."

I wondered why they all had hired me. The only one whose motive was clear was the first, Mrs. Bordeaux. She was suffering. "You'll do it, won't you?" she had said to me. "The doctors won't. My daughter won't. But you will, Jillian." She was right. She taught me something about myself—something I still don't fully understand.

Father brought me back to the present. "Is Dobb going to let you get away very often?"

"Theoretically, I'll have one day a week off. But she sleeps a lot. I can slip out most days for an hour or two, I think—to see what you need."

"Don't worry about my needs. I think Mrs. Tickle wants to help with those. But she can't help with the biggest one: my need for my girl Jillian."

Father reached an arm out to me, and I placed my hand in his. "Miraculous," I said.

In his days of tent-church revivals, the promotional flyers had referred to "The Miraculous Healing Touch of Matthew Cole."

"What's miraculous," Father said, "is how much hassle it's caused me. Right from the start. When I was twelve, I had a newspaper delivery route . . . have I told you this story?

"No."

"I keep thinking you know everything about me."

"I will someday."

One of the pleasures of my life was that I was getting to know my father at a time when I had enough tolerance and understanding to allow me to accept him. If I had known him when I was a child or an inexperienced adult, I would probably have been embarrassed or repelled by his behavior. He wasn't just eccentric; he had a blend of eccentricities that I had still found outlandish when I was reunited with him. But I was thirty then and was beginning to find that outlandish people were more appealing and often more benevolent than those who were conventional. Too many of our conventions are camouflage for selfish impulses. My grandmother, who raised me, was a conventional person. And she regularly diverted money from her church's missionary fund into her own substantial investment holdings.

Father resumed his story. "One of the great American educational processes was the paper route. I'll bet they still have the classical form of them in Serena: the kid (girls now, too) with the bicycle and the canvas bag full of folded papers. Collection day was when you really learned things. You learned about the strange attitudes people have toward even small amounts of money. You got to see and smell the insides of your neighbors' houses. I hated collecting the weekly payment from Mrs. Faye because she would take my hand in both of hers and sit with me the way you're doing now. I was too polite to say no. Her husband had to walk in on us, of course; accused me of screwing his wife. I didn't deny it because I wasn't sure what screwing included; I thought maybe hand-holding might be part of it."

"It should be," I said.

Father wasn't interested in my opinion. "There was talk of sending me to reform school," he said. "I felt used and guilty at the same time."

"What about the unfortunate Mrs. Faye?"

"I have no idea. It didn't occur to me that I could have sympathy for an adult. I put Mrs. Faye out of my mind and vowed to keep my hands to myself in the future."

"And how long did you keep your vow?"

"A few months. Until my first miracle."

"Miracle?"

"The miracle of the sandlots—a healing. I was playing third base in a gym-class baseball game. There was a force play at second; the runner and the kid playing second base got tangled up in the slide, and the runner's leg got broken. The gym teacher went to call an ambulance, and I went over to the boy who was hurt—a friend of mine. When I touched his leg, which was a swollen purple mess, his pain stopped, and by the time the teacher got back, the leg was back to normal."

"Who called it a miracle?"

"The teacher called it that. The kid who was hurt wasn't sure. And everyone else said the teacher had been imagining things."

"And what did you think?"

"I knew damn well it was a miracle. And I hoped it would never happen again."

"You're still hoping that, aren't you?"

"Yes. Oh yes."

"Don't worry. I'll protect you. I'll keep you in the world of the commonplace."

Father laughed and then said, "Is that where we are?"

"Of course. We're in the heartland. We're with Mrs. Dobb and Mrs. Tickle. Everything's safe and normal."

I poured us some more coffee. While I was up, I put a tape on Father's little portable cassette player. It was a tape he had made of his own piano playing—a long improvisation on Billy Strayhorn's "Chelsea Bridge."

Father and I sat side by side, holding hands and listening to jazz as dusk fell over the heartland. Two happy Americans.

4 | *Signing a Contract*

I was seated across a desk from Mrs. Dobb's son, David, in the walnut-paneled study of her house. "I like old people," I said.

"I don't believe you, Jillian. No one likes old people." Mr. Dobb was the kind of man who calls all women by their first names. He was also, I suspected, the kind of person who sees all women—if not all other people—as his victims. "Old people are repulsive," he continued. "Particularly poison-tongued old people like my mother—as you'll soon find out." He handed me a three-page contract. "This makes you our slave."

"Your *mother's* slave, I hope you mean."

Mr. Dobb displayed a strained smile before saying, "You're probably wondering why I'm not subjecting you to an elaborate interview, why I'm not trying to gauge your character." He didn't give me time to respond. "Actually," he continued, "I'm hoping you're a person of weak character; at least, I'm assuming you are. So I've taken a precaution in the contract. It stipulates that you cannot be rewarded for your duties in any way except through the designated salary—no bequests, no gifts."

"And no sexual favors?"

Mr. Dobb's head moved back in surprise. "Delightful," he said. "Nothing's forbidden in that area. The document's concerned with the sin of avarice, not lust."

"Then you believe in sin?"

"Certainly. Sin is when you do something I'd rather you didn't do."

"What about crime?"

"That's more complicated." Mr. Dobb paused for a moment—a sign that he was becoming more serious. "The plug, for example. If my mother were dependent on a life-support system, would you pull the plug?"

"I can't answer theoretical questions. When the circumstances are right, people do things they hadn't imagined they could do." Mr. Dobb seemed satisfied with my answer. "Let me ask *you* a question," I added. "Are all Dobbs obsessed with death?"

"There aren't many of us. Perhaps that explains our morbidity. We see that the end is near for the family. We're just hurrying the process along; I'm certainly doing all *I* can to help."

"Your mother said you have a twin."

"Yes. But you'll be disappointed in her. She's rather healthy-minded."

"And your mind isn't healthy?"

"It's fashionably unhealthy. I was a forerunner of the yuppies—a proto-yuppie—narcissistic, greedy, shallow. Now I'm showing them what to do with their money. They dote on me, recognize me as a pioneer."

I wondered how accurate David Dobb's self-assessment was. Totally accurate, probably. He took excellent care of his body—keeping it healthy and dressing it tastefully and expensively. And even though he obviously could be sexually aggressive, I got the impression that if you gave him a choice between a weekend in Venice with the most exciting woman he had ever seen and advance notice of a corporate takeover, the woman would have to find someone else to share her gondola.

There was something off-putting about this man. There was a layer of confusion under his self-assurance and a lack of authority in his reedy voice.

31

I glanced through the contract, but I knew that the words on the paper were less important than the words that were in David Dobb's mind as he watched me.

I looked up and smiled at him. "I guess it's all right. I'll trust you, Mr. Dobb."

"David," he said. "And I *hope* you'll trust me." He got up and stood next to me, his thigh against my arm. "I'll show you where to sign." He took my hand and guided it to a signature line on the last page of the contract. I signed quickly and stood up, backing away from him.

"It's too bad about Mrs. Ellis," David said.

"Mrs. Ellis?"

"Your last employer. I understand her death was unexpected. And I *also* understand her son John has been trying rather peevishly to find you."

I couldn't think of anything to say. David was warning me, and I was sure my expression showed alarm. His expression was tinged with triumph.

I wondered how he could have learned of my previous employer so quickly and just exactly what he knew. Could he have traced me to some of the positions I had held before my time with Mrs. Ellis? How much would he tell me? "I don't seem to have any secrets from you," I said.

"Good friends shouldn't have secrets from each other."

"But your whole life is a secret from me."

"What would you like to know? Ask me three questions. You'll see how guileless I am."

I wanted David Dobb to go away, but plainly, if I were going to be his mother's companion, I would have to learn to deal with him. Just as I had learned to deal with Mrs. Ellis's son. I might as well play David's little game, even though I was not sure of the rules.

"Question number one," I said. "Do you love anyone?"

David didn't hesitate. "Certainly not. I'm not even vaguely fond of anyone. There was a time when I was quite fond of myself, but it turned out to be a passing infatuation."

I suspected that despite his flippant tone, David was being honest. "Do I disappoint you?" he asked.

"No. I don't trust people who love or who want to love. But I'm supposed to be the questioner. Question number two: Is there anything you wouldn't do for money?"

"Obviously. Otherwise I would have a lot of it instead of being in danger of falling into the middle class . . . I won't do anything that's likely to get me put in prison. Money is meaningless if one is not free to misuse it. Next and last question, please."

"Would you inform on a friend?"

"On a friend, yes, but not on an accomplice."

"Then since we're not accomplices, I think I'd better leave Serena—before John Ellis arrives."

"I wouldn't hear of it, Jillian. We need you here. I expect you to make all our lives . . . richer. I don't think there's any chance that Mr. Ellis will find you as long as you remain with us and help us with our needs. On the other hand, if you were to leave, there's a good chance that Mr. Ellis would catch up with you."

I moved across the room and considered David's threat. He was a formidable opponent, and perhaps I should have left town and taken my chances on his not bothering to pursue me. But it was likely that he was underrating me. I doubted whether it had occurred to him that *he* might have reason to be apprehensive. He was grinning confidently at me.

"I'm late for an appointment," he said. "I'll stop on the way out and ask the housekeeper—whatever this one's name is—to show you your room. It used to be my room; I thought you'd like to know that. And think it over . . . can't we just be accomplices?"

* * *

The room I was to live in was splendid. There were actually three rooms: a large bedroom, a sitting room, and a bathroom, all of them ornate and shabbily comfortable. Although there was electric wiring throughout the house, Elizabeth Dobb kept kerosene lamps in the bedrooms, preferring, as I did, the softer light of a flame.

I have never lived in rooms that haven't been lived in previously by others. I enjoy looking for the signs of a former life: the nail clipping or Christmas-tree needle lodged in a crack in the floor; the ghostly rectangle on the wall where an unimaginable photograph or painting once hung. And in these rooms, the former life was David Dobb's. This was where he lay in the darkness making the decisions that shaped his unpleasant personality; this was where he learned of his body's odd needs.

The rooms were similar to those I had grown up in—the rooms in my grandmother's house, where I was sent to live after Father left home and after Mother lost interest in me. Although I often thought of Granny, I had never decided whether I should think of her with resentment or gratitude. It was probably true—as she had announced to me each day—that she loved me. But it seemed to me that people often use their love as an excuse to mutilate the loved one's life.

That evening, as I sat with Mrs. Dobb, I said to her, "You never loved your children, did you?"

She didn't seem to find the question presumptuous. "One of them, perhaps. Briefly. But now I can't be bothered."

After a moment, she added, "I think I could love you, Jillian."

"Please don't bother," I said.

5 | *Mrs. Ellis and How She Died*

I couldn't forget David Dobb's warning that John Ellis was pursuing me. Several times each day, as I stood in my room or walked along the hallway, I paused, convinced that John was standing behind me. I held my breath, I felt an odd tingling in my forearms, and I turned quickly . . . only to find that I was alone.

What was most disturbing was that when I imagined John's presence I couldn't decide whether he wanted to accuse me of being responsible for the death of his mother or whether he wanted to demonstrate his love for me.

John was attracted to me from the moment we met, and his mother had expected that I would marry him. She was given to making sentimental statements, the most embarrassing of which was to call us Jack and Jill and to say we were destined to live together. I'm not sure she took into account the fact that the nursery-rhyme characters' life together was not very placid or romantic.

Although John was personable and physically attractive, there was something peculiar about his shambling strength and perceptive gaze—something implying that regardless of what you expected of him, he would disappoint you. This quality was connected to his late mother's enormous capacity for disappointment. During my companionship with Mrs. Ellis, I spent hours each day listening as she recollected the disappointments of her life. I think it was this process of recollection that brought her eventually to beg me to put an end to the disappointments. "*You* won't disappoint me, will you, Jillian?" she would ask on sleepless nights. She would take my hand and brush her dry lips across the knuckle of each finger. Then she would place both my hands on her neck with my thumbs against her windpipe. "You're strong enough to help me, aren't you?" she asked.

"Physical strength isn't required, Mrs. Ellis. Courage is what is needed—courage and the knowledge of where to place a slight, undetectable pressure on the carotid arteries. In moments, the brain starves; the system shuts down."

"And you're a courageous woman, aren't you, Jillian?"

"I have been courageous when I thought it was necessary."

"Is this one of those situations?"

"Yes."

Mrs. Ellis grinned for the first time since I had known her. I could see that there had probably been years early in her life when her smile had been frequent and imposing. She said, "Isn't it odd that you have the courage to help me in this way, but not to help me by marrying my son? Why is it that women find him unacceptable?"

"He doesn't allow for uncertainty."

"I think I know what you mean. That's why he chose that ridiculous profession."

John was a minor-league baseball umpire. He made a living taking part in a game—a game he understood well but played badly. And he had to assume that every event was right or wrong; that every pitch was either a strike or a ball; that every fly ball that dropped along the line was either fair or foul. More than most people, I know that no one wants to be judged on those terms. And so, although John Ellis pursued me with charm and devotion, it was his mother's needs—not his—that I responded to.

Inevitably, the night came when Mrs. Ellis welcomed me to her bedside for the last time. She was holding a folded garment, and there were tears in her eyes. The tears were not a sign of fear or grief but of ecstasy. It was not the first time I had seen such tears in an old person's eyes.

Mrs. Ellis unfolded the garment she held and handed it to me. It was a simple, white cotton short-sleeved tunic. "It's a gown I first wore on an important night—a night that was more important than any other," she explained.

"Your wedding night?"

Mrs. Ellis smiled broadly. "No. That night was not high on the list."

The tunic was limp from wear and repeated laundering, and its whiteness was faintly yellowed.

"Would you put it on, my dear?" Mrs. Ellis asked.

"Now?"

"Yes. It would be appropriate."

I went back to my room and quickly changed from the robe and gown I had been wearing. The tunic's thin material had become translucent, and my nipples, which I've always found dissatisfyingly large and dark, were evident. I pulled the short skirt closer to my thighs, and the dark triangle of my pubic hair appeared clearly. But despite the sexual suggestiveness of the gown, its simplicity also gave me an appearance of innocence. I felt like a child who was about to take part in an important ritual.

When I returned to Mrs. Ellis's room, she said, "Charming. You look angelic."

"I do feel innocent . . . but not virtuous."

"There are many kinds of angels, Jillian, just as there are many forces acting on our lives. You'll realize that someday."

Mrs. Ellis was basically a religious person, although not in a conventional way. Her son John said she was a saint who had made a wrong turn at some point in her life. Since the death of her husband, she had spent most of her time sitting in darkened rooms, apparently deep in thought. As her companion, I had shared many of those hours with her. In the beginning, I thought she was dozing at such times, but then I realized that she was extremely alert. She seldom left the house, but she corresponded with several women, writing each day to at least one of them. Although on the surface her life was passive, she created a sense of intense, contained energy, as if she were conserving and channeling a force—perhaps one of the "many forces" she thought I would understand someday.

"I never think of there being forces to serve," I said. "I simply serve companions."

"We are all shaped by the same forces, but we don't all realize it."

At most times, I would have discouraged such a conversation, but this was a special night. I could not deny my companion the opportunity for her last words. Nevertheless, I had no need of her forces. I had always taken responsibility for my own actions.

"Come here, my dear," Mrs. Ellis said. She touched my tunic. "I wore this for the first time on the night that my husband left me. I have never had a happier night. For the first time in decades, I slept free of his strange pawing, free of his sour body. It was a rededication. I became virginal again. It was worth everything to me. *Everything.*"

I found it difficult to look at Mrs. Ellis. Excitement had transformed her features. In a sense, she looked youthful, but the youthfulness was distorted by emotions that young people cannot experience—emotions that even I, her companion, could only guess at.

"You don't understand, do you, Jillian?" Mrs. Ellis asked.

"No."

"You will understand soon. Think of me then. Think of me and the others you have helped."

Mrs. Ellis took a small white leather box from among the bedclothes. She opened the box, revealing a tangled cache of rings. She withdrew a ring that was set with a large diamond, and, taking my hand, she placed the ring on my third finger.

Then she produced, one by one, seven other rings, all set with large precious stones. Weeping and murmuring incomprehensibly, she placed one ring on each of my fingers. Some of the rings turned loosely on a finger, and others would not go beyond the first joint.

When I was wearing all eight of the rings, Mrs. Ellis sat up and took my face in her hands. She placed her lips on mine. I tasted the salt of her tears.

I grasped my dear companion's shoulders and lowered her onto the bed. I placed my hands over her eyes and closed them. I kissed each lid.

Then I placed my ring-garish hands upon her throat. She looked at me and smiled. "Yes," she said. "Yes."

Within a few moments, I had made another human being happy.

I kept the white tunic and the large diamond ring, and occasionally, on sleepless nights, I would put them on and watch the ring gleam in the firelight as I paced about my room considering the strangeness of life.

6 | *My Dinner with the Dobbs*

During my first week with Mrs. Dobb, she spoke only of her family. She spoke favorably of those who were dead and harshly of those who were alive.

"Confused and useless," she said. "That's what the Dobbs are. This century has defeated us. We've lost the nineteenth-century knack of being dignified and evil. We no longer understand exploitation. We've forgotten why the U.S. Constitution is such an admirable document: it allows us to exploit one another and our environment with dignity. But we've lost our nerve."

"Perhaps you're being unfair to your children. You can't blame them if they're only reflecting the times they live in."

"A superior person rises above the times. My offspring are not superior. You've met David. As you might expect, his twin, Eva, is not any better. She's worse, actually, because she has the traditional woman's proneness to inviting men to degrade her."

"Have you seen your daughter recently?"

Mrs. Dobb grunted and shook her head no.

It was a bright morning, and the strong, flat light filtering through the curtains of the bedroom revealed a pinkness under Mrs. Dobb's usual pallor. She was enjoying the chance to criticize her children.

"Perhaps it would do you both good to see each other," I said. I was concerned less with bringing Mrs.

Dobb closer to her daughter than with arranging an opportunity to meet the younger woman myself. "You could give a dinner party," I said.

"A party?" Mrs. Dobb seemed offended by the suggestion. "I don't give parties, my dear."

"You should, though."

"Why should I, Jillian?"

"Because you're the mother, Elizabeth."

It was the first time I had used Mrs. Dobb's first name. She stared at me, almost smiling. I allowed her to stare. She looked exceptionally alert in the morning light, and it was obvious that her mind was moving quickly; not wandering aimlessly, but going from point to point like a hunting dog following the scent of an elusive prey through underbrush. Eventually, she simply said, "It's time to get out of bed."

The state of Elizabeth's health was a mystery to me, as it apparently was to everyone else, including her doctors. Her heart had a structural weakness of some kind, but the problem's effects were unpredictable.

"What about your heart?" I asked.

"My heart does as it's told; it's not to be taken seriously."

Shaking off the hand that I placed under her elbow, Elizabeth threw the covers back and swung her legs over the side of the bed. She went to the center of the room and assumed her best posture. Through her half-transparent nightgown, her body seemed remarkably attractive except for a thickness around the abdomen.

"Come here," she said. "Stand with your back against mine." I kicked off my slippers and moved against her. She said, "Our bones are similar. Our legs are the same length."

It was true. Although I was about three inches taller than Elizabeth, our buttocks met at the same level; my extra height was in my torso and neck. Elizabeth moved around to face me. She rested her toes on mine, wriggling them occasionally. She placed her hands on my waist. "Your waist is what I envy. It's not slender, but it curves inward. A woman cannot be seductive without a waist of some sort."

"Is there someone you want to seduce?"

"No. But one should be prepared. Especially if one begins giving parties."

I wondered whether I would want to be prepared for seduction when I became Elizabeth's age, and if I was prepared for it now. I had never gone out of my way to make myself attractive, and I imagined I would be grateful when the seducers finally began to look at me with indifference.

Elizabeth took my hand and led me to one of the room's three full-length mirrors. We looked at each other's reflections. No one would have mistaken us for mother and daughter. We were from different stock. It was unlikely that any ancestor of mine had ever employed a servant—or had ever been one. I looked crude and self-sufficient. My body was not something to be displayed but something to be discovered, pleasantly, beneath heavy fabrics. Elizabeth's body was meant to be half seen through a peignoir. I wondered if, in the Victorian age of invalid wives, some women had chosen that life because they looked their best in bedjackets.

As we gazed into the mirror, Elizabeth slowly stepped backward and moved behind me, standing rigid and close. She maneuvered so that she was no longer visible to me. "I have vanished within you," she said, and then slowly moved back into my sight. "And now I have been reborn from within you. I've taken some of your youth."

"You're welcome to it," I said. I wondered if that was what I had begun doing with my life—giving my employers bits of my remaining youth, offering them a rebirth into death.

Elizabeth and I exchanged a glance in the mirror. "Maybe you are beautiful after all," she said.

"A case of the eyes of the beholder," I said.

Elizabeth turned to face me directly. "It's *your* eyes that give the impression of beauty." She paused, and I sensed that her moments of seriousness had ended. "But you may be one of those persons who use their eyes as instruments of deception. What color are they, would you say?"

"Gray-green."

"And your hair?"

"Gypsy black."

"It *would* be helpful, I suppose, for my family to meet my gypsy friend socially."

I smiled. "I could tell their fortunes."

Elizabeth telephoned her children and arranged for them to come for dinner on a Saturday night and stay at the house overnight. I was to arrange the details with our housekeeper, Mary Hess.

Mary arrived every morning except Sunday at seven o'clock. She was as careless about her own appearance as she was about the appearance of the Dobb house, and she had a constantly puzzled expression. Someone who didn't look closely might dismiss her as ugly and stupid. It was possible that I was one of the few people who had ever taken the trouble to look closely at her.

Mary prepared three meals, shopped for food, and did some uninspired housecleaning. Describing herself as a modern cook, she microwaved an odd, plastic-trayed repertoire that Mrs. Dobb called "airline food for nonflyers." The prospect of cooking a formal dinner upset Mary, and the thought of what she might serve upset Elizabeth. As a compromise, Mary suggested that we hire her brother Larry, who was the cook at a nearby restaurant and was trying to establish a catering service. Larry and I made the arrangements by phone. I assumed he was competent because he was enthusiastic and because I had never heard of most of the items on his suggested menu.

Mary was pleased by the arrangement. She said, "You're bringing a new sense of life to this house, Jillian."

"That's what I'm here for, Mary."

"Where are the men?" Elizabeth Dobb asked.

We were seated around the large oak dining table. Besides myself, there were Elizabeth, David, Eva, and Eva's daughter, Shirley. Eva, David's twin, was an architect whose business had recently failed and who had left her husband. She was discovering the meaning of irresponsibility and happiness, according to her mother. Eva's daughter, Shirley, was unsettlingly beautiful. A recent college dropout, she had, also according to Elizabeth, always known the meaning of irresponsibility but not of happiness.

The dinner was going well. Larry Hess had produced a puzzling but enjoyable meal, and as often happened at family gatherings, the pleasing sense of shared origins was overcoming personal antagonisms. But Elizabeth was right: where were the men?

David responded to her question. "I'm assuming you were trying to offend the ladies and not me, Mother. If there is anything I'm secure about, it's my masculinity."

Actually, after several predinner scotches, David seemed less clearly masculine than before. What there was no doubt about was his sexuality.

"Don't protest too much, David," his mother said. "What I meant was that the women at the table don't seem to be able to hold a man."

Eva said, "Either we aren't able to or we don't *want* to, Mother." Eva was remarkably similar to David in appearance. They both had auburn hair and brown eyes and were the same height—about five feet eight inches. I thought that if David did have any problem with his masculinity, it must have grown out of being constantly confronted with a female version of himself in his childhood.

Elizabeth said to Eva, "Remind me, dear. Are you divorced or only separated?"

"Divorced, Mother." Eva had hesitated before answering, as though she were not sure it was proper to talk about her failed marriage. She also lit a cigarette —something she had done every fifteen minutes or so throughout the evening.

"Do they still require grounds for divorce? Did you have to accuse the man of something?"

David interrupted. "The wearing of bad clothes, I would imagine."

Eva ignored David—something else she had done throughout the evening. It occurred to me that she had probably not looked at her twin more than once since she had arrived.

"It's true, Eva," Elizabeth said. "Your husband did dress appallingly for an architect."

"He wasn't an architect," Eva answered. "He was a builder. I'm the architect."

"When this house was built," Elizabeth said. "we didn't make such distinctions."

"Obviously," David said.

Elizabeth looked at David with contempt. Eva ground out her cigarette on her plate. I got the impression that Eva and her mother were closer than their conversation indicated. Eva turned to me, still uncertain of whether I was her friend. "What do *you* think of the house, Jillian?"

"I like its texture more than its shape."

Eva considered my statement. "I think I agree," she said. "Are you interested in architecture?"

"No. I've never been interested in anything except people."

"Have you studied them? Psychology or sociology?"

"I've never been interested in studying."

Shirley looked at me with interest for the first time. She said, "You've just lost some points with the family, Jillian. They all think they're so fucking smart."

"Oh, I'm pretty fucking smart, too, Shirley. I just don't like to study."

"Speaking of fucking," David said to me, "you aren't married, are you?"

"Not now. I was."

"You found your husband lacking?" David asked. He had just emptied his wine glass and was having trouble enunciating.

"I just found my marriage unrewarding. It was an unrewarding relationship in every way."

David produced a malicious little grin and said, "Jillian probably finds relationships with old people more rewarding in every way. Have there been some bequests, my dear?"

I was disappointed in David Dobb, even though my expectations hadn't been high. I thought he was going to use his knowledge about my background to greater effect than simple dinner-table innuendo. I had expected him to limit himself to some elaborate form of emotional or financial blackmail.

Mrs. Dobb said to me, "You'll have to excuse David. He's obsessed with the idea of inheritance."

"Of noninheritance, actually," David said.

I tried to lighten things up. "Is that an inherited trait?" I asked. But this was apparently a subject that the Dobbs didn't treat lightly.

Eva said, "David and I are living evidence that there are serious exceptions to any theories about inheritance of traits. We couldn't be more different."

"You exaggerate, Eva," David said. "We still have a

few things that are comparable—things that most people might find identical."

Eva was flushed with anger. The emotions that lay between these two people were obviously exceptional. Eva and David had been aware of each other and probably resenting each other since before their birth. Side by side in the womb, they must have developed a resentment at having to share that intimate space. They could just as easily, I thought, have each developed a gratitude to the other for furnishing companionship in that darkness.

Elizabeth, who was seated between the twins, intervened with practiced assurance. "Behave yourselves, you two," she said. She reached out and put her hand on Eva's, turning away from David. Then she said to me, "Be thankful you never became a mother, Jillian . . . or am I making a false assumption?"

"No. Circumstances never seemed right for that."

David said to his mother, "You're Jillian's child, Mother dear. She would like you better if you were wearing those adult diapers they promote on television—you don't wear them, do you?—and if you talked the kind of goo-goo nonsense babies talk instead of the pol-polysyllabic nonsense you *do* talk."

Elizabeth was too experienced with David's abuse to show any anger. "Polysyllabic? That's an offensive and incomprehensible accusation."

Everyone smiled. But they were probably wondering, as I was, whether there weren't some elements of truth in David's comments about me. One of my companions had been reduced by aging almost to a second infancy, and it had given me a particular pleasure to care for her. But as was true with my other companions, I had not chosen that woman. Each of my companions had chosen me. I was fulfilling her needs, not my own.

Eva was looking at me sympathetically after

David's little attack. She said, "Your father lives in Serena, doesn't he, Jillian? You should have brought him along tonight."

If Eva knew that Father lived in Serena, she must also have known he was blind. I supposed she was just trying to be discreet and let me know she was sympathetic.

"Matthew has terrible table manners," I said.

"Matthew?" Eva asked. "Matthew Cole? I knew someone with that name. One of our firm's first commissions was for a church—or a tabernacle—in Illinois. Matthew Cole was the reason I accepted the commission. He was the only person in his organization who seemed honest . . . and he was the only one with any concept of spatial beauty."

"That sounds like my father. But he has trouble with spatial beauty now."

"I must see him again," Eva said. "Could you call him now and ask him to come here for a drink after dinner? You can use my car to pick him up." Eva was clearly yet another woman who found Father unforgettable.

Elizabeth was intrigued by Eva's enthusiasm. "We'd all like to meet your father, Jillian. Won't you ask him if he would like to join us for coffee and cognac?"

"If you insist," I said. But I wasn't pleased.

After dessert, I excused myself and telephoned Father, who, as I expected, was unable to refuse cognac and was ready for a little relief from his atonement. As I was speaking to him, I saw Shirley wander into the kitchen and begin to talk to Larry Hess, the handsome chef. David Dobb was staring at me invitingly from across the room. Elizabeth had lost all traces of her pallor.

I was frowning.

7 | *A Wager Is Made*

When Father arrived, there was a blossoming of the emotions that had begun to appear at the Dobbs' dinner table. It was obvious why he had been so effective as part of fundamentalist services.

He smiled benevolently and passionately during the introductions. He said to each woman, "May I take your hand? It helps me to visualize you." Supporting the woman's hand on the palm of his left hand, he let his right hand skitter lightly over each finger, tracing outlines, grazing the gentle tumescence of veins. I found the display embarrassing, and I was relieved when David received the traditional firm, one-handed clasp.

Eva sat next to Father on the sofa and spoke to him about the tabernacle she had designed. Elizabeth, making no attempt to join the conversation, stared at Father in undisguised fascination. I kept the cognac glasses full. Soon, no one was speaking.

Father was probably aware, as I was, that too many of us were without partners and that the undirected, cognac-charged emotions were likely to bring family antagonisms to the surface.

"When the words stop, the music should start," Father said. "Are there any records or tapes in the house?"

Elizabeth and the twins looked at one another.

Eva said, "Father had some records. They're probably in the attic."

49

David said, more vehemently than he should have, "No one's been up there for years. Let's not get involved in that." I suspected that David might have been up there not too long ago.

Elizabeth looked at Father apologetically and said, "Perhaps some other time, Mr. Cole. You may stop by anytime. Jillian could look through the things with you."

"Would there be any jazz records?" Father asked.

"Quite likely. Most of them are from my husband's college days in the late twenties. Jazz was unavoidable then."

"It still is," Father said.

"Not in Serena, Mr. Cole," David said. "Everything of any vitality is avoidable here."

"Don't you believe it. And call me Matthew. Are you a betting man, David?"

David looked amused. "Of course not."

"Well, pretend you are. I'll bet you my diamond ring against a case of J W Dant bonded that there's jazz being performed right now within ten miles of Serena and that there will be a church service tomorrow morning within the city limits that would bathe your eyes with tears of joy."

Everyone was smiling, but the smiles were nervous. I said to Elizabeth, "Father gets carried away." Then I turned to him. "Remember, dear, not everyone shares your interests."

"They'd have a better time if they did." Father turned his head in David's direction. "Is the bet on, David?" he asked. As he spoke, he pulled off his diamond ring.

David said, "How much does a case of J W Dant cost?"

"Less than this," Father said, and threw his ring to David. The throw was remarkably accurate, and what seemed just as remarkable to me was that David caught the ring without apparent effort.

"Every small-time faith healer and second-rate piano player has to have a large diamond ring—large and flawless. That one is six carats with a rare lavender cast to it. I don't suppose it's something you'd want to wear in public, but there's a type of client who would respect you more if you did."

David laughed. "The bet's on," he said.

Elizabeth said to him, "I knew your greed would overcome your sense of decorum."

Father said, "And, Elizabeth, I hope *your* sense of decorum will allow you to come pub-crawling and church-going with us."

Eva, who was still sitting next to Father, looked alarmed. She said. "It's not a matter of decorum but of health, I think. Mother's heart wouldn't react well to that sort of thing, Matthew."

"Nonsense. There's nothing safer than traveling with a healer." Father's old professional charm was reviving. He looked in the direction of Mrs. Dobb. "Elizabeth," he said, "come sit next to me."

I was about to object, when Elizabeth surprisingly pushed herself to her feet and, waving Eva aside, sat next to Father. She took his hand.

Thirty minutes later, six of us were in David's Cadillac, our moist, cognac-scented breath blending with the arid breezes of the heating system and the smoke from Eva's cigarette.

I sat in the front seat between David, who was driving, and Shirley, who had become sullen at having had to leave her new acquaintance, Larry Hess. David's arm was heavy against mine, and occasionally he produced an annoying twitch of his bicep. In the back seat, all was right with Father's world. He was flanked by strong-minded, attentive women, one about fifteen years older than his sixty years and the other about fifteen years younger. He was fulfilling one of his precepts, which said that happiness was obtained not by improving one's personality but by finding the right setting for it.

The conversation was dominated by Elizabeth and Father. If I hadn't known Father so well, I might have thought he was seriously attracted to my new companion. I, unlike Elizabeth, knew that although he seemed to be reveling in her company, he was actually indifferent and would have responded in the same way to Mrs. Tickle or to a stranger sitting next to him on a bus. One reason he appeared to like people was that they were all the same to him. Blindness had made Father more self-absorbed. Recently, he had said jokingly about people, "They all look alike to me."

"Don't you miss having a real home, Matthew?" Elizabeth asked. It seemed like an unsubtle and premature remark, but I had seen other, more severe women react the same way.

"I'm from frontier stock," he said. "Gotta keep on a-rollin'." Father's parents had come to the United States in the late 1920s to escape the poverty of industrial northern England (and to find the poverty of the U.S. Midwest). That seemed to me to be a loose interpretation of the term *frontier stock*. But maybe not, from what I knew of Detroit in the years of the Great Depression.

Eva said to her mother, "Maybe a sightless person doesn't become as fond of buildings as we do."

"Is that true, Matthew?" Elizabeth asked. "Do you become fond of a building's sounds . . . or of its smells?"

"A building's just a space. I don't get excited about space—not in the way I do about sounds. The reason I wouldn't have a guide dog, for example, is that a dog's bark is the ugliest sound ever devised."

David said, "How do you feel about canes? I notice you don't have one of those, either."

"They're quiet enough. Tap tap. But luckily, I've got

Jillian, who makes pleasanter noises, to take care of me."

David said, nastily, "I understand Jillian has taken care of a number of people. Were they all as grateful as her father?"

Elizabeth answered calmly, "I'm sure they were, David. I am *certain* they were. Just as *I* am grateful."

David turned to me and said, "It's fun while it lasts, is that it?"

"Fun isn't what I supply," I said.

"No," said David. "I gather you offer something more permanent."

Fortunately, I didn't have to reply. We were pulling into the parking lot of a roadhouse seven miles east of Serena. According to Larry Hess, who had recommended it, the roadhouse was known locally as Walter's, although its purple neon sign announced, dramatically, "WALPURGIS."

8 | *A Hand on My Shoulder*

We could hear the music as soon as we opened the car's doors. The instruments seemed to be piano, guitar, and bass, and the melody was something I knew was written by Thelonious Monk, although I couldn't recall its title. Father had won the first half of his bet.

Eva helped Father out of the car, but then she slid into the back seat again, next to her mother, and said, "Maybe we should wait here for the others. You could have a little nap."

"Are you trying to protect my health or my sensibility?" Elizabeth asked.

"Taverns are nothing you ever cared for, Mother. It would be a pointless strain for you."

Elizabeth looked at her daughter with tenderness, as if realizing that Eva's concern was genuine. "It's not pointless, dear. It's foolish. A nap would be pointless."

Eva and I helped her mother out of the car and walked on either side of her. We took her arms, but she shook free of us. David guided Father. When we got to the entrance, Elizabeth said, "This used to be the Daytons' house. John Dayton never came home from the Second War, and Edna was taken advantage of—financially—by her lawyer. She never cared for music."

The old house—a mansion, really—had been cleverly adapted to its new function. Part of the floor at ground level had been broken away, and what was formerly the cellar was now a sunken area for dancing. Surrounding the dance floor at ground level was a horseshoe of boxes in an opera-house arrangement. An elevator led from the back of the dance floor to a third level: a dimly lit, circular mezzanine containing a series of rooms that were, I assumed, used by amorous visitors.

Our party drew a great deal of attention, most of it amused but some of it disapproving. The host, who led us to our box, tempered his welcoming smiles with anxious glances at Elizabeth, who looked especially vulnerable and frail in these surroundings. Once we were seated and had ordered champagne, however, Elizabeth's expression took on confidence and dignity. Soon, she was looking out at the room with the air of a reigning dowager at a charity ball.

The place was crowded, but it was not particularly noisy, partly because of good acoustics and partly because the people were paying attention to the music. Although most of the clientele was young, their long hair and 1960s-style clothing made them look middle-aged.

Father quickly became oblivious to everything except the music, and within ten minutes, Elizabeth and Eva began to look bored, tired, and perhaps a little jealous. Their enthusiasm had been for Father's company and not for nightlife.

As Elizabeth's energy dissipated, I began to feel more comfortable. I found her looking at me occasionally with longing, as though she wished we were in her quiet room and that I were listening attentively as she told me about her life as an adolescent or as a young bride. In the bluish, low-level lights of the roadhouse, her face now looked unlined but exhausted, as it might have looked after she gave birth to Eva and David.

David's spirits were rising. Like me, he was more

comfortable with his mother in the role of a semi-invalid. He said to Father, "I'm not sure that you've won your bet. How do we know that the musicians are playing jazz and not just cocktail music?"

"Does the music soothe you?" Father asked.

"No. It makes me edgy."

"That's because it's jazz. Cocktail music would make you want to sing."

"There have been jazz singers, haven't there?"

"No. That was the name of a movie. You can be sure that if someone is singing, it's pop music, not jazz."

I knew that under pressure Father would admit that Louis Armstrong and Billie Holiday had sometimes sung jazz, but basically he was being honest.

David may not have been soothed by the music, but he was apparently stimulated by it. The champagne also helped.

Shirley had excused herself and was now moving provocatively about on the dance floor, although it wasn't clear whether her dancing was a solo or whether one of the young men squirming in her vicinity was her partner. Shirley was a pleasure to watch. Unlike many dancers who merely try to look erotic or athletic, she was also trying to move beautifully.

Eva and I were sitting on either side of her mother, and soon we both drew close to her. Eva's attention moved back and forth between Elizabeth and the building's odd interior. Eva obviously had more affection for her mother than for the building. I said, "There's something disturbing about the house, isn't there?"

"What's disturbing about it is that it's a whorehouse. It's a case of form reflecting function . . . degrading function, degraded form. But it's lively."

I looked more closely at the mezzanine level, with its circular array of rooms. Although occasionally people could be seen emerging from the elevator at the

the head of the circle and moving along the corridor, their identities were obscured by an arrangement of mirrors and trellislike screens. It was like watching ghosts moving along a street balcony in New Orleans.

Elizabeth said, "This is a world I didn't know existed this close to Serena."

"Are you pleased to know about it?" I asked.

"Yes. I'm glad to know people are not devoting all their energies to crops and primness. I'm glad to know that there is decadence as well as dullness."

"Let us know when you want to leave."

"We should stay a while. Matthew is more than pleased. But don't be concerned if I don't try to make conversation."

The trio had begun to play a more relaxed number. "Minor blues," Father said. He always announced the chord structure or name of a tune and was irritated if it was something he couldn't identify.

David got up and asked me to dance with him but didn't give me time to reply. He pulled me to my feet and guided me unsteadily to the dance floor. Once he had me in his arms, however, he moved gracefully and steadily. There was a disquieting delicacy in the way he held me.

Shirley was now standing next to the bandstand and was looking with unconcealed interest at the pianist who led the trio. His name, according to a sign on the stand, was Charlie Blake. His eyes were closed, but even if they had been open, he wouldn't have seen Shirley; his concentration on the music was absolute.

David didn't seem to want to make conversation, but there were a few things I wanted to straighten out between us. I asked, "Am I going to see much of you, David?"

"Of my body, you mean? I hope so."

I ignored his adolescent reply, which I assumed resulted mostly from the champagne but also partly from sexual immaturity. Unlike Eva, who seemed completely at ease with her body and its needs, David appeared always to be trying either to restrain an impulse or to exaggerate one.

"Relax, David," I said. "Relax in my arms." I had the sense that I was the one doing the holding. "We have to reach an accommodation of some kind. No cynicism; no indirection. If you can't make some kind of honest statement to me now, I'll leave Serena. I have to know what you want from me."

"You mustn't leave. I don't want that." David seemed to be sincere, but I knew he was a person who was seldom sincere. He was also a person who preferred asking questions to answering them. "Maybe you can tell me first what you want from my mother," he said.

I remembered that when Elizabeth had asked me that question, I had said I wanted her life. But I couldn't say that to David. I was silent.

"You see, you don't really want honesty. You just want to be free to play your ghoulish games."

I pulled away from David, but he gripped my hand painfully and said, "I won't stop you, my dear. Just let *me* play, too."

"You don't know the rules."

"Teach them to me."

"You have no talent for this."

"For what?"

"For what I do."

"You're afraid to put a name to it, aren't you?"

I wouldn't. I couldn't.

David smiled. "I have many talents. I might surprise you."

I suspected that any surprises David had for me would be unpleasant and that his major talent was for an old-fashioned activity: villainy.

Our conversation ended. I had drunk enough champagne so that the motion of dancing combined with the reflected images in the mirrors around the dance floor were disorienting to me. One image in particular began to disturb me—an image I had seen not too long ago, but one I couldn't define. David was guiding me in a circular movement that brought the same images to me again and again. (His hand was also making little excursions to my supposedly erogenous zones.)

The image that was disturbing me was that of a young woman. She was not dancing but was standing in a shadowy area, talking to a man whose back was to me but who also seemed familiar. I could see only their reflections. The woman eventually looked up and caught my eye in the mirror. I immediately remembered where I had seen her; she was the woman who had been sitting at the bar in Plaines while Father and I were waiting for the taxi to take us to Serena. I got the impression that the woman had also recognized me and that she was telling her friend about me.

"Let's leave," I said to David.

"You look distressed," he said. "More than could be explained by my mediocre dancing or my discreet groping. So I accede."

As we walked away from the dance floor, I felt the notorious gesture that we all live in fear of: a hand was placed firmly on my shoulder.

I turned to find myself looking into the eyes of John Ellis, the son of my previous companion. His expression had the same intensity that his mother's had before she closed her eyes for the last time.

9 | *Night Thoughts*

"I've been looking for you," John Ellis said.

I couldn't think of a reply, so I distractedly introduced David to John, even though I wasn't sure they hadn't already met. "John's mother was my previous employer," I said to David.

David nodded.

I said to John, "David's mother is my new employer."

"Where?" John asked.

"In Serena," David said.

I wouldn't be able to escape John Ellis now.

"I hope your mother is well," John said to David a little too pointedly.

"She is."

The two men stared at each other with challenging curiosity.

"I hope she stays that way," John said. "Mine didn't."

Then he turned his aggressive gaze on me. I thought, it's a look he perfected in his silly profession. Theoretically, John Ellis was a bigger threat to me than David Dobb. John could ask the authorities to investigate his mother's death and perhaps had already done so. And although it was unlikely that they would have found any irregularity in her death, an investigation could have disrupted the modest routine of my life. Yet, as I compared the two men, David

Dobb seemed the more threatening despite his more delicate body and blasé manner.

If John presented a threat, it was sexual. Hovering in the background was John's barfly woman friend. I wondered whether she had visited the mezzanine with him, but my curiosity wasn't strong enough to make me want to investigate the matter. John had once told me that he often patronized prostitutes as the result of being on the road so much and his need for at least one orgasm a day. He spoke of this appetite not proudly but with a touch of embarrassment. And he soon demonstrated the truth of part of that claim to me.

"We have to go now," I said.

"Say hello to your father for me," John said. "Tell him I'll be dropping in."

I took David's arm and led him away for a moment. I was grateful that his arm was available.

As we walked away, I thought I heard John Ellis say, "Jack and Jill." I didn't look back at him, but I remembered that his mother had hoped we would marry.

The musicians in the trio were taking a break when we got back to our table. Father was being attentive to Elizabeth and Eva. Just as David and I arrived, Shirley appeared, leading the pianist by the hand. "I want you all to meet Charlie Blake," she said.

Father said to the young man, "You sounded good, but you put too many measures in the minor blues."

"Not too *many*," Charlie said. "Just more than usual." Charlie looked surprised that anyone had been analyzing the structure of his music, but he apparently wasn't surprised enough to want to discuss it. He was slender and pale, and I wondered if he had an interest in exotic powders and pills. He didn't seem interested in Shirley or any of the rest of us—which was a change I welcomed. Charlie pulled free of Shirley, waved vaguely at us, and walked away. I envied him his freedom and honesty.

Now that the music had stopped, the voices in Walter's were becoming unpleasantly loud. Conversation became a decibel contest. I began to notice odors—ragged plumes of pot smoke drifted by, blended with a fetid aroma that I assumed originated in the rooms of the mezzanine. There seemed to be more contrast in the lighting; the dazzling beams of tiny spotlights penetrated the overall murk.

David and his sister began presenting alcohol-enhanced reminiscences of their childhood. But, curiously, they spoke not to each other but to anyone else who was available, whether the other person was listening or not. The similarities in their appearance seemed to grow stronger as they spoke. Occasionally, I had the illusion that they had exchanged clothing and identities. And I thought it likely that such an exchange had taken place more than once in past reality.

Father had knocked over his wine glass, and Elizabeth was on the verge of unconsciousness. Her head was slumped forward, and her mouth was opened slightly. I hoped she was merely sleepy and not ill. Her hand was resting on Father's forearm, but he seemed too confused to notice her.

Across the room, John Ellis and his woman friend were standing together, smiling and talking. Their eyes were on me.

I wondered how we had come to be in this night-marish situation. I woke Elizabeth and helped her to her feet, getting no help from Shirley, who was at the table but had been watching Charlie Blake and was only marginally aware of the rest of us. "Tell the others your grandmother and I will wait in the car for them," I said.

Elizabeth seemed alert once she was standing, but she was weak, and she leaned heavily on my arm as I led her to the car. She was trembling violently.

After I started the engine and turned on the heater, we got into the back seat. I took my coat off and draped it over Elizabeth's legs. Then I took her into my arms. Her trembling subsided. She's mine, I thought. Her surprising, acerbic intellect and her flirtation with Father meant nothing. She had given in to the desire we all must face eventually—the desire to spend our last months as we spent our first months, in the arms of an affectionate, devoted woman.

Elizabeth and I had left the others behind in the noise and contention. There was a warm, moist patch between my breasts where Elizabeth's breath filtered through the silk of my blouse. I looked away from the gaudy roadhouse, across the frozen earth, and into the darkness. My eyes stung with tears.

No one slept well in the Dobb house after our Walpurgis outing. I didn't even bother to go to my room. I sat next to Elizabeth's bed, responding to her occasional remarks and listening as her children and grandchild tossed in their beds or paced about in their rooms, their smallest movements revealed by the floor planks which had the responsiveness of a piano's soundboard.

"You were offended," Elizabeth said.

"Yes . . . and worried."

"It was your father's doing."

"People overwhelm him. They always have. We should leave him to his music."

"He's life-enhancing."

"That's not what you need, Elizabeth."

"No. But it's disquieting to encounter it for the first time at my age."

"Yes. But it's not what you need," I repeated.

"No."

"What is it you need?"

"I need you, Jillian."

"Yes."

Elizabeth and I needed each other, just as my other companions and I had needed each other. I recalled the moment when I first decided to become a companion. It had had the suddenness and urgency of a religious conversion. It was not as if I had made a decision about the future course of my life, but as if I had been called. Each of my companions had welcomed me as if she had spent her life in preparation for our brief friendship.

It occurred to me that too many people did not hear when they were called; too many people were not prepared to take extraordinary action. Ours was a timid age which was cut off from many vital traditions. How many were willing, as I was, to dedicate themselves to the forces of friendship and death; to stand modestly and alone in obscurity; not seeking the encouragement or rewards of an organization or the notoriety of the media?

It disturbed me to be thought of as a bad person. People are too willing to see badness. They see it in blameless creatures; they shoot the hawk which has no choice but to drift in circles, poised for minor, efficient destruction, helping to maintain nature's design.

I didn't think of myself as anything as grand as a hawk, but I knew I was part of a design.

As I waited for dawn, I thought once more of John Ellis. He was a man who, as he had told me often and smugly, was in the right place at the right time. "The way I see it," he had said, "there are four things Americans are really good at: baseball and jazz, which they invented; and faith healing and serial murder, which they perfected." John's misfortune was that he couldn't play any of the four games that interested him. He sought consolation by becoming a professional observer of one of them: baseball. He sought out Father for information about the second and third of his interests. At that time, he mistakenly thought that I wasn't able to teach him anything about any of them. But that opinion might have changed. Nevertheless, like a good American man, he had expected me to help him with his fifth interest: sex. I helped him occasionally, because I'm an American, too.

Why had John Ellis followed me? What was he seeking? Nothing classically theatrical, like revenge, I supposed. The baseball field was John's theater. Some kind of ill-considered emotional blackmail was more likely. But I reminded myself not to underrate John.

Sometime before daylight, I heard a distant tapping on the door of my unoccupied room and the sound of David Dobb's voice speaking my name. I remembered the odd sensation of being in his arms when we had danced together. I decided I never wanted to have him in my bedroom, and I wondered if his charm was simply camouflage for some kind of freakishness of desire.

10 | *Come Sunday*

Before dropping Father off at his rooming house the night before, we had arranged that David and anyone else who was interested would pick him up at nine-thirty on Sunday morning to settle the second half of the bet.

I was the only one interested in the expedition. Elizabeth, Eva, and Shirley were unwakable. David pleaded a champagne headache and said he was willing to concede the bet by default.

I insisted that David honor his commitment. I brought black coffee to his room in a mug with a bendable straw so that he could drink without raising his head. I filled an enormous ball-and-claw-footed bathtub with warm water and, to lure David out of bed, offered to scrub his back for him. Fortunately, he refused my help and managed to bathe on his own.

Father had relied on Mrs. Tickle for advice on which church service to attend. Father's first choice was always a Baptist service presided over by a black minister. But there weren't many truly black people in Serena. The few nonwhites I had seen seemed dispirited, their ill-defined features and pigment reflecting imperfectly the passion of an earlier generation.

"What you try to avoid," Father says, "are preachers who talk in tongues; they literally don't know what the hell they're talking about. What you look for is good music. A good preacher is basically a singer—someone who wants to make some pretty noises."

The Companion

When I went to pick up Father that morning, I hesitated outside his door. Coming from his room was the sound of an operatic recording—a duet or trio of women's voices. It was an unlikely sound to hear from Father's room. His tolerance for opera was not great; he was not interested in nonmusical elements such as the libretto or the staging or performer worship. And too often that left too little to admire. The door of the room was slightly ajar, and I knocked softly and pushed it open. The music was subsiding after a climax that seemed beautifully lyrical and controlled to me. Mrs. Tickle and Father sat side by side, not touching, listening with an intensity that kept them from noticing me. Mrs. Tickle was weeping. The music continued to subside, and one of the women sang the German words, *Ja, Ja,* in what was, judging from Mrs. Tickle's sobs, a poignant moment.

The orchestra swelled up to a conclusion, and we were left with the sound of the landlady's emotion—which was seldom expressed, I imagined. When she became aware of me, Mrs. Tickle quickly recovered her reserve. The opera was Richard Strauss's *Der Rosenkavalier,* and the *Ja, Ja,* had been the words of an older woman losing her lover—something that Mrs. Tickle's explanation made sound truly tragic. It didn't seem like an ideal time to take Father from her, but at least it would just be a temporary separation. Eventually, the separation would be permanent, and I wondered how Mrs. Tickle would react then.

The Come Sunday Baptist Church had at one time been something else—just what it had been was not clear. It stood isolated at the edge of a field just inside town. It was too small to have been a barn and too long and narrow to have been a house. David thought it had been a two-story poultry house and that the upper floor had been removed. When I pointed out that people seemed to like to alter buildings in Serena, David said he thought it was called thrift.

There were about fifty people seated in the church when Father, David, and I entered and settled ourselves in a back pew. Although most of the congregation were black or brown, we were not the only white people attending. Father wanted to know if there were lots of fat ladies smiling and wearing hats. There were, and he said that was encouraging.

There was also a choir consisting of four men and four women. The only musical instrument in sight was a chipped white-enameled upright piano.

The white-suited preacher entered from the back of the church and walked slowly up the aisle, smiling and greeting members of the congregation. He looked as self-satisfied as a bridegroom. He was a large, soft, brown man who obviously dealt in excessive emotion. As he entered the church, a young woman had unobtrusively seated herself at the piano and had begun to play the blueslike melody of Duke Ellington's "Come Sunday." One by one, the choir members began to hum the tune, and by the time the minister had taken his place before the altar, the sound was intense enough to set up vibrations in the building's loose, unfinished floorboards.

While the minister stood with his head bowed, the choir hummed one more chorus of the melody, gradually becoming quieter, until the final notes were barely audible. Father and David seemed moved and respectful. In fact, David seemed to have a tear on his cheek, a tear that I assumed was more a result of his hangover than of religious fervor. I raised Father's hand to David's face and placed a finger on the tear to let him know he had won his bet.

Whatever David thought of the ceremony, I found it cheaply theatrical.

The preacher did not stand in a pulpit or behind a

lectern. He paced before the altar like a neurotic polar bear.

The sermon began quietly and informally.

"I want to talk about something you don't want to hear about. Nobody talks about it. Everybody pretends it's gone away. But it's still here. You know it is. It's death."

There was a stirring among the congregation, particularly among the members of the our little party.

"The Supreme Court—although in my mind it's not quite supreme—says it's okay to die. We've got a right to die. Those wise people say it's okay sometimes to pull the plug."

I remembered David had used that phrase when he interviewed me.

"If you're using *extra*ordinary means to keep your granny alive, you can stop if you want. Praise the Lord, you can stop. Does the Lord care?"

The preacher paused and looked out at his congregation. I didn't get a sense that anyone knew where the sermon was headed. I had an idea of what might lie ahead, and I was glad Elizabeth wasn't with us.

"Does the Lord care? No, the Lord doesn't care about *extra*ordinary means . . . because *none* of His means are ordinary, they're all *extra*ordinary. *Life* is *extra*ordinary. And the Lord doesn't care if you die in a burning automobile . . . or from a raging cancer . . . or from a pulled plug. The Lord only cares that you are His when you die."

Some "Hallelujahs" were murmured in the congregation. The preacher's prowling was becoming more restless, and his voice was louder and less comprehensible.

"The Lord may let someone heal you, or He may let someone take your *extra*ordinary life away from you. What I want you to understand . . . what I am here to tell you—"

"Yesses" rose from the congregation. The black people of Serena were less dispirited than I had thought.

"What you must understand is that *when* you die or *how* you die . . . whether you're a drowning child or a plug-pulled ruin . . . doesn't matter. What *matters* is that you die for the Lord . . . with dignity . . . and innocence . . . and Christian devotion."

The minister's voice was now transformed into a feral wail. People were beginning to stand and respond.

"Better to die unplugged . . . one with the Lord . . . than to live outside His grace . . . unwashed by His cleansing blood. So I say, pull your machine plugs . . . get plugged into the Lord. Into the *Lord*. And how do you do that? That's what I'm here to tell you. Hallelujah."

The congregation was so noisy by this time that it was difficult to hear the preacher. Father believed what the preacher said was secondary. What mattered was the way he said it. His sermon was becoming a wordless song. David was still caught up in the service, although I had no idea why someone with his cynical, sophisticated attitude would find it anything but amusing. Father seemed to be amused but professionally interested. Then the preacher said something that interested *me*.

"And *how* do you get plugged into the Lord?" he screeched. "With your *soul*. Your soul is the plug. But *you* don't do the plugging; the *Lord* does that. . . . Now, if you have an understanding of plugs, you know that there is a male and a female in that world, too . . ."

Apparently, I wasn't the only one whose attention was caught with this metaphor. The chorus of "Amens" and "Hallelujahs" became more moderate, and there was some nervous laughter.

"And the Lord is the male . . ."

Of course.

"And your soul is the female. You just—praise God—have to lay back and open up your soul . . ."

There was an expectant silence in the congregation.

"Just lay back and let the Lord plug in."

The congregation responded with a trumpeting of cries. David got to his feet, and for a moment I thought he was carried away by the excitement. But then he pushed past me and left the church. I took Father's hand and led him toward the door, but I was moving slowly and listening to the sermon.

The preacher was saying, "Now it sounds so simple; it sounds so easy. But you can't be easy with the Lord. If your soul is easy, there's another power that is going to plug into it . . . there's the power of evil . . . there is Satan."

As we left the church, I heard, over the commotion, "Don't let your soul be easy."

Father was grinning. "Not bad," he said. "But we didn't wait for the collection. That looks cheap and rude."

He was right. I asked David and Father to wait for me, and I reentered the church. The sermon had ended, although its excitement continued in the hymn singing that followed. I put fifty dollars in the collection plate. After the service, the minister took my hand at the door. I said, "My friend sends his apologies. He wasn't feeling well."

The preacher was displaying a mechanical after-service grin, but there was a serious intelligence in his eyes. "I affect a lot of people that way," he said. "And besides, Christianity is an acquired taste."

"What about evil?" I asked.

"I'd say we all have a natural taste for that, wouldn't you?"

"Some more than others."

"Oh yes. The easy souls."

The minister released my hand. I walked sullenly to

the car, feeling guilty but not knowing why. I asked David why he had left, and he said he had felt an attack of the giggles coming on. But I—and Father, too, I knew—remembered David's tear.

Mrs. Dobb's son, I concluded once again, was subject to odd emotions.

11 | *Talking to the Twins*

Preachers are deceptive. The good ones deceive only themselves; the bad ones deceive us all. Preachers understand universal fears, but they don't understand that some of us have overcome those fears. Some of us see death, for example, not as extinction or a gateway to another life but as the natural culmination of life—a flowering. Elizabeth and I understood that.

After we left the church, David and I delivered Father into the eager custody of Mrs. Tickle before returning to the Dobb house. David seemed unaccountably concerned about Elizabeth, and when we got home he went to her bedroom while I was taking my coat off. I met him on the stairs as I was on my way to Elizabeth's room. "She looks dreadful," David said. "I was worried enough to offer to take her to the hospital to have her heart checked. But she refused. 'It's not my heart,' she said. 'It's my soul.' She should have heard the sermon."

I remembered that Elizabeth had spoken about taking my soul. "That would have made her even more upset," I said. "The sermon was vulgar."

"I'm not sure," David said. "I lost my bet with your father. I was moved at first."

"You were hung over. And I noticed you left during the most offensive part—about the male and female plugs and letting the Lord—or Satan—put his plug into one's soul."

"Oh, I suppose people who know about such things

73

might see that as sacrilege. But I simply thought it was silly. And I gather the congregation wasn't offended."

"No. That's why I'm not a member of a congregation."

I found Elizabeth sitting rigidly in a corner of her bedroom. As David had led me to expect, she looked ill and uncomfortable. She was wearing only a cotton nightgown, and the room was cool.

"There's no need for you to be up," I said, and I went to her bed and straightened the bedclothes. I was suddenly aware that I was also tired, and I thought longingly of my own bed. I settled Elizabeth under the blankets and stroked her forehead, watching the color gradually return to her face. Eventually, she opened her eyes. I was afraid she might blame me for not having been with her when she awakened. But instead, she said, "I'm sorry I couldn't be with you this morning."

"That's all right, Elizabeth. You had a right to be tired. We all did. And the church service wasn't soothing. It was stimulating at times, but I think it was intended for people who had slept long and soundly on Saturday night. It was a substitute for revels."

"Yes," Elizabeth said. "There is little difference between the sacred and the profane. They're both exhausting."

"Shall I read to you now?"

"For a few minutes. I'll be asleep soon."

"Would the Bible be appropriate?"

"It never seems appropriate to me—all the blood and violence. The Bible seems like a man's book to me. Maybe modern women are attracted to it, but I'm a throwback to the age of the gentlewoman. I prefer the bloodless world of Jane Austen."

I went to the bookcase and took out Jane Austen's *Emma,* a book I had never read. Most of the women I had served had liked Austen's *Pride and Prejudice,* but

I never knew why. I found the people in the book silly and the author's language stilted. But I realize I'm not a cultured person. I'm too American for that.

I began to read from Chapter 1 of *Emma:*

> Emma Woodhouse, handsome, clever, and rich, with a comfortable home and happy disposition seemed to unite some of the best blessings of existence; and had lived nearly twenty-one years in the world with very little to distress or vex her.

I didn't identify with Emma. I wondered if Elizabeth Dobb would like to be introduced to the novels of Raymond Chandler.

Elizabeth was soon asleep, and I couldn't blame her. I took her pulse, which was erratic but not alarmingly so, and I went downstairs. Eva was in the parlor, apparently waiting for me. "Do you have a minute?" she asked.

I sat down and watched her pour a large helping from a bottle of scotch. It was a brand I'd never heard of and couldn't pronounce. I assumed it was expensive because of the plainness of the bottle and its label. Eva handed the glass to me, but I shook my head no. She drank half the glass eagerly but without the look of satisfied concentration that a devoted drinker shows. She held up the glass and said, "This is one of the things that have come to seem important to me recently."

"Is your mother another of those things?"

"Yes. Mother's important now; my ex-husband is not. Scotch is important; my job is not."

"You've lost interest in architecture?"

"Not in architecture—just in my self-worshiping contribution to architecture. I used to believe that buildings were more important than people. I could get sexually aroused more easily by a barrel-vaulted church nave than I could by a barrel-chested man. I still tend to think that Shirley was conceived not by my husband but by the dining room of Sir John Soane's house in London. Do you believe that, Jillian?"

"Of course not. I think that's what Father calls horse buns. You're like your brother and your mother. You like to dramatize."

"And maybe you like dramatics—maybe that's one of the reasons you're here. But I'm more interested in the other reasons you're here." The whiskey was bringing a pinkness to Eva's white skin, covering the faint freckles that were left from the summer.

I said, "I'm here because your mother wants me to be here."

"I suppose that's true, and Elizabeth should have what she wants. But I wouldn't like any harm to come to her."

I couldn't tell whether Eva was implying I might want to harm her mother. I assumed Eva had talked to David about me and that he might have given her some kind of warning about me. I decided to ignore that possibility. "Who would want to harm your mother?" I asked.

"She's fragile. Anything could harm her. Last night, for example. The strain of that silly excursion could have killed her."

"She wanted to go; no one forced her."

"Your father forced her."

"Nonsense." It sounded as though Eva were jealous of Father.

"He forced her indirectly. I think your father is a dangerous man."

I tried unsuccessfully to stifle a laugh. I had thought Eva was more perceptive than to believe something like that. "Father is an innocent," I said.

"Yes, he's innocent; that's his danger. He has a power, and he's naive."

"What do you know about his power?"

"I was just guessing . . . generalizing. What do *you* know about his power?"

I would have preferred the Dobb family not to know Father's background, but Eva had trapped me. "He has the power to heal," I said. "It's a power he doesn't want and that came close to destroying him."

Eva drained the last of the scotch from her glass. "You and Matthew aren't a pair of loonies, are you?"

I smiled and shook my head.

"No," Eva continued, "you're something other than loony. But you are dangerous. I'm going to ask Elizabeth if she would mind if Shirley and I came to live here for a while."

I smiled again—graciously, I hoped. "How nice," I said. And I thought, *You want to take my job away. You're pathetic. You've botched your own life, and now you're looking for new fields to botch.*

Eva turned her head and stared—probably unconsciously—at her whiskey. Then she stared at me with the same look of attraction and resistance. "I love my mother, Jillian."

"I'm sure you do, Eva."

"Even though I knew I was her favorite, she never seemed to give enough of herself to me. There were periods—sometimes months—when we were close, but I always had the feeling there was something in her life more important to her than I was. Children sometimes can't accept that. But I can accept it now. I want to make my love available to her."

I began to feel more sympathetic to Eva.

She continued, "I thought you might be experiencing something like that with your father. I thought maybe he could heal my mother—give her a longer, healthier life."

"I'm not sure that's what your mother wants."

"That's what everyone wants, Jillian; you really don't understand that, do you?" Eva got up and left the room.

She shouldn't be allowed to design buildings, I thought.

I went upstairs to check on Elizabeth and found her sleeping with such intense stillness that I immediately reached for her wrist. Her pulse was stronger and more even than it had been when I left her earlier.

When I returned to the parlor, I had a moment of confusion. David was sitting where Eva had sat earlier. His legs were crossed in the same way as hers had been, and he was drinking scotch from the same glass she had used. I wondered whether they had arranged the dramatic little substitution to unsettle me or whether it was the kind of echoing behavior that twins are supposedly subject to naturally.

"I thought you were Eva," I said.

"There are times when I think that, too. When we were children, we looked more alike than we do now—a great deal more alike. Mother never dressed us alike, though."

"I don't understand," I said. "Why would she dress you alike? And would she have dressed you both as girls or both as boys?"

David blushed. "You see how confusing it is to be a twin," he said. "What I meant was that I would dress in Eva's clothing on my excursions to steal cookies from the kitchen, hoping that if someone saw me, they'd think I was Eva."

I enjoyed seeing David's discomfort, and I decided to extend it. "I assume you've lost your impulse toward cross-dressing?" I said.

He seemed ready for the question. "I have, yes . . . sorry to disappoint you."

"And what about your impulse toward letting other people take the blame for your misbehavior—or your crimes?"

"Oh, I do that, of course. How could I make a living

otherwise? That was one aspect of my childhood experience that served me well."

"You must have been an unpleasant child."

"And you think I'm an unpleasant adult, don't you?"

"I don't know you well enough to be sure—and don't want to. But I'd guess that you're without principles and that you will go to extremes. But you're not without charm, of course."

"Is this a proposition? Do you find unprincipled men appealing? Shall we slip up to your room?"

It's a pose, I thought. *He doesn't want me.* I was certain that if I accepted his offer, he would pretend it had been a joke. I stared into his amused eyes for a moment, and then I realized that I found Eva more attractive than David; her beauty was somehow more honest than his handsomeness. I decided not to give him the satisfaction of imagining that I might get sexually involved with him.

"It's not a proposition, David. You'll never get a proposition from me. I simply said you aren't without charm. I could have added that it's the kind of charm—like a TV weatherman's—that I find the opposite of arousing."

"Unkind," David said. But he didn't look hurt. If anything, he seemed relieved. "Unkind," he continued, "but not surprising. We know you are capable of spectacularly unkind acts."

"One person's spectacular unkindness is another's act of mercy."

David looked at me with his peculiar intensity—a type of intensity I hadn't encountered before. And even though I had meant it when I told him that I wasn't attracted to him, there was still something fascinating in his combination of decorum and passion. He was wearing a dark three-piece suit. The vest was fully buttoned (except for the bottom button, which I supposed was left open not for comfort but on the advice of his fashion coordinator). Yet there was a completely unbuttoned look in his eyes. I suppose he was an example of the corporate pirate—a person playing abstract games with the economy and Wall Street to satisfy his urges toward pillage, rape, and murder.

As I expected, what David—like Eva—really wanted to talk about was Elizabeth. "You're fond of my mother, aren't you?" he asked.

"I suppose that's hard for you to understand."

"No. I realize she can be attractive to people who haven't had the misfortune of being raised by her."

"Your sister doesn't agree with you. She's planning to come and live here—to help take care of Elizabeth."

David rolled his eyes upward and parted his lips. I had given him an unpleasant surprise. "Eva has no more use than I have for Mother. She's just looking for a refuge." David finished his drink in one slow tilt of the glass. Then he smiled at me faintly and said, "Is Eva's presence going to alter your plans a bit?"

"I doubt it."

"I'm glad to hear it. I'm on your side, you know. That is, I approve of your goals, though I don't pretend to understand your motives."

"Maybe you think my father and I are just a pair of loonies."

"Probably. But that's not what's important. The important thing is whether you're evil."

"*Dangerous* is the word Eva used. She thinks my father is dangerous."

"If Eva comes to live here, perhaps you could fulfill her sense of danger—add her to your activity list. Or is she on the young side?"

I felt my stomach tighten with anger. It was time to end the conversation. "Eva's undeserving but not too young. She's no younger than you, David."

12 | *A Séance*

I looked in on Elizabeth once more and discovered that she was still in a profoundly deep sleep. She probably would not awaken for hours. I didn't want to take a chance on being forced into another encounter with her children, so I left a note for her and went to spend some time with Father.

I needn't have worried about Father's being lonely or disconsolate, however. I found him still in a social mood, this time as a host. He was entertaining Mrs. Tickle. When I knocked on Father's door, there was a pause before he asked me in. When I entered, the room, he and his guest were seated decorously on opposite sides of the room, although I got the impression that Mrs. Tickle had just made a hasty move across the room. I was sure that the chair seat beneath her ample buttocks was still cool.

Sarah Tickle was handsomer than I had remembered. She was like someone in northern European mythology who undergoes a trial or is on a quest. She was about five years younger than Father, in her mid-fifties. Her long gray-blond hair was painstakingly braided and wound in a circular arrangement at the back of her muscular neck. The tall solidity of her body was tempered by a sensuousness I hadn't noticed before.

I greeted the landlady without enthusiasm and sat next to Father on the sofa. As I expected, the cushions next to him were warm. I was offended—not because of Mrs. Tickle's presence but because of her petty deception.

Father seemed to be enjoying their little game. "Mrs. T's been telling me about our auras," he said. "Mine is yellow, and yours is purple."

Who cares? I thought. I didn't share Father's interest in the occult and the supernatural. He agreed with me that such phenomena are irrelevant to the business of day-to-day life, but he found them a fascinating diversion. What amazed me was how frequently we encountered people who believed in paranormal events. If pressed, almost everyone seemed to be willing to confess harboring a belief in fortune-telling, extrasensory perception, spirit messages, or any of the dozens of other activities I thought of as either silly or fraudulent. I wondered if Father, with his apparent talent for faith healing, attracted would-be psychics and prophets.

I said to Mrs. Tickle, "I'm afraid I don't know the usefulness of an aura."

"It helps to gain insight into the true nature of oneself, Miss."

There was the slightest indication of what I took to be a German accent in Mrs. Tickle's speech—a touch of "z" in the "th."

"And I have a purple nature?" I asked.

"You have a great, dark strength—I would say, an affinity with negative forces."

I looked at Father and became aware of one of the great drawbacks of trying to communicate with a blind person. I wanted to give him a "Do we have to put up with this?" glance, but instead I would have to be more direct and less polite. My affinities were really not her business. But rather than say something rude to Father's guest, I decided to ignore her.

I said to Father, "Elizabeth was exhausted. I thought I'd see how you were doing."

Whatever Mrs. Tickle's special powers of perception were, they did manage to pick up the message that I wanted to be alone with Father. "I should be going," she said.

Father, however, seemed to prefer his Rhine maiden's company to mine. He asked her to stay, and he outlined her history to me—a history that was dreary but not undramatic. Mrs. T's name was Tickle to her neighbors and lodgers, but officially it was Tüchel. She was sent from Germany to Serena as a child just as World War II began and was raised by relatives. Her parents disappeared in Europe during the war. She married, but her husband was killed in the Korean War. She inherited his house, took in boarders, some of whom (the more timid, I imagined) she persuaded to attend discreet séances she conducted.

Father seemed to find Mrs. Tickle's history fascinating, and he eventually admitted that they had "joined hands" with each other and had "experienced each other's power."

How nice for them.

"But we'd like to try it with a third person," Father said.

"Try what?"

"Just a little joining of hands around the table. Interested, sweetie?"

"Not really. And you'd probably have better results with someone who's more sympathetic."

Mrs. T said, "It's your aura that's most important. You would do well."

"Let's try it, Jillian," Father said.

So we tried it. We went to Mrs. T's apartment, which had a spacious parlor that featured, exactly in the center of the room, a round, highly polished mahogany table. Mrs. T drew drapes across the windows, placed three chairs around the table, and lit three candles in sconces along the wall. We sat down.

"What do I do?" I asked.

"Just relax, Miss," Mrs. T said. "Relax, and we all

join hands. We will be silent for a time. I will seem to sleep, and then I will speak. But the voice and the words will not be mine. If you become disturbed or frightened, release my hand."

I was already disturbed, annoyed with myself for letting Father persuade me so easily to take part in whatever this was. "Is this a séance?" I asked.

Mrs. T nodded and looked at me with an authority that had only been implied previously. It was not the maternal domination of a stern landlady but the seductive control of a sensual woman. She took my hand, and I gasped. It was like receiving a mild electric shock, but without pain or unpleasantness. It made me realize it had been months since I had experienced, or had wanted to experience, an orgasm.

"Ooooweee." It was Father's noise of delight. He had taken Mrs. T's other hand.

I didn't want anyone to speak. I didn't want to play hocus-pocus. I just wanted to enjoy, for as long as I could, this new emotion—an emotion that I could only think of as sexual. How much of religion, or pseudo-religion, was based on sexuality? I wondered. Father claimed that people in the world of fundamentalist, pentecostal religions often confused religious emotion with sexual emotion. Many of the people he healed, Father said, were just feeling relieved at having someone touch them sympathetically. Sex is what's miraculous, he said.

Mrs. T, as she had warned us, seemed to fall asleep immediately. She might have been pretending, but it was a convincing performance. Her head slumped forward, and her breathing became slower and deeper. The grip of her hand relaxed.

I also began to relax. People want someone to touch them, Father had said. My hands were being touched by two remarkable people. I felt secure. I was soon aware only of my hands; hands that, like my Father's, knew an art; hands that had quickly and gently brought peace and comfort to the women I had served as companion.

A gurgling moan began to issue from Mrs. T's throat. It was a moan I had heard on certain nights, a moan of finality. I suddenly felt naked, and an intense sensation of heat and tingling began to move from my hands, up my arms, across my chest, and down my abdomen, settling at the joining of my thighs in a surge of warmth and moistness.

The moan continued but began to break up into sounds that resembled poorly formed words. And then the sound in Mrs. T's throat became a name: "Antonia." It was the name of my first companion. My confusion and arousal increased. Was I imagining things? Had I simply heard the words I wanted to hear in the noises Mrs. Tickle was making? She spoke again: four syllables that *could* have been "Antonia." It had been months since I had thought of Antonia or of any of the other companions I had lived with before Mrs. Ellis and Mrs. Dobb. It wasn't that I had not been devoted to them all or that I found it unsettling to think of the past. It had never been my habit to think of the past—or to speculate on the future—unless forced to do so. And the séance was confronting me with the past. I remembered words that were so significant to me, words spoken in Antonia's high-pitched, uninflected voice: "It's time you learned not to fear death, Jillian. Death—my death—will bring you life." Those words had seemed silly and puzzling to me at the time, but they were prophetic. Antonia's death reshaped and recharged my life.

Mrs. T was speaking again. This time, she uttered three syllables, which I heard as "Miriam," who was my second companion. She had been grateful to me for bringing about the only event she had ever looked forward to in her long life: its ending. I heard her feebly spoken words: "I need to make my pain useful or to end my life. Jillian, can you help me do either of those things?" I couldn't think—then or now—of a way to make pain useful. However, I was able to assist her in the act she lacked the means or courage to commit.

Mrs. T continued to make indistinct, guttural sounds, and it occurred to me that she might have been speaking German. But my recollections had become independent of her words. She might have inspired my thoughts, but she was not supplying the words I recalled.

There were four others whose presence and words returned to me.

Jessica—obese, ill, and middle-aged—was the only one I had disliked, the one who in the final moments made me feel not just virtuous but pleased. "We're the part they threw away, Jillian," she said. "Let's take our revenge together." I declined Jessica's invitation to join her. I didn't feel discarded, and my concept of revenge was to do something to someone else and not to myself. But I helped her toward her own goal and wondered if in doing so I was also being vengeful in some complicated way.

Nancy's husband had wanted me to be the one to share the private world she inhabited. He said, "You might as well call her what I call her: Skitzy. She thinks it's a term of affection. She's still quite affectionate in an abstract way . . . as am I, my dear." He put his hand on my thigh and added, "It's her mind and not her body I've been deprived of." At Nancy's request, I saw to it that her husband was deprived of her body, and I was tempted to deprive him of his own.

Janet had said, "I have always been a bon vivant. When life ceases to be bon, one must cease to be vivant. But I am also a dedicated coward, Jillian, and I must hire your courage." Death, Janet taught me, can be a test of a person's frivolity.

Nora represented more specifically than my other

companions a belief that many of them have shared: "We who have grown old in a harsh landscape have learned the lesson that has evaded those who retire to the false nurture of Florida: Life should not be preserved at any cost."

A tightening of Mrs. T's grip brought me back to the disconcerting present. Had one of us been speaking during my reveries? Mrs. T's grip relaxed slightly, and she said, apparently to me, "The changeling will be the next." I waited for her to explain, but she only repeated the words: "The changeling." Then she pulled her hands free of mine and Father's. She raised her head and opened her eyes. The candlelight seemed brighter. Mrs. T stared straight ahead as if confronted with something either unbelievable or distasteful or both.

Then her gaze softened. She turned first to Father and then to me, smiling as if she were slightly embarrassed.

"So?" she said.

"You were impressive," I said. And I thought, *but to what effect?* I was moved, but only as I would have been by an impressive passage in a book or a scene in a movie. It was finally just an entertainment in which I had done most of the work—a self-entertainment.

Father reached out toward Mrs. T. She gave him her hand again. His hand moved upward. He leaned toward her and squeezed her upper arm. "Fabulous," he said. "You coulda been a contender." Mrs. T smiled uncomprehendingly. I hoped they weren't going to become more than just friends and fellow occult power brokers.

And I wondered if and when I would meet the changeling.

13 | *A Cosseting Touch*

When I returned to the Dobb house in the early afternoon, I found Elizabeth waiting for me. She was looking stronger and calmer than she had in the morning, and I began to feel an emotion I often felt with the women who became my companions: a kind of shared peacefulness that seemed to originate not within either of us but in the room we inhabited.

"Would you like to get up?" I asked.

"No, dear."

"You're still feeling weak, then?"

"Not at all. I'm just feeling neglected. I need cosseting."

"I'll try to help you, Elizabeth. But I'm not certain what cosseting consists of."

"Pampering. But the commercialists have taken that word from us. Or you might say that cosseting is simply the supplying of companionship. But I'm hardly an expert on the subject. I've seldom been offered companionship. I was asked for it occasionally by friends, but I got the impression that what I offered was not adequate."

"Did that upset you?"

"Not in the least. If it was a problem, it was my friends' problem."

"Your husband never expected companionship?"

"Not from me. But I only knew him when he was sexually active. I think it's children and old people—

sexually inactive people—who crave simple companionship. Am I right? You're the expert, Jillian."

"I'm the companion, but I'm not the expert. I don't analyze my experience. You may be right. The old and the young are more likely to be satisfied with the mere presence of someone. Lovers and family members want to practice their emotions."

I doubted whether Elizabeth was as simple and undemanding as she pretended. She might, for example, be sexually inactive, but judging from the interest she showed in Father, that might mean only that she lacked opportunity—not desire. I didn't resent her pretense, though. It allowed for surprises.

We sat for a few minutes as the cold, early winter light faded. Then I drew the curtains and lighted the lamp. I realized that Elizabeth's preference for lamplight was not just sentimental but was also a matter of esthetics. The room was designed to be seen in a warm, dim light that cast deep shadows. The mausoleumlike quality I formerly saw in the room was less apparent. All the textures were heavy: wood carved in highly raised relief, brocaded and hand-crocheted fabrics. There was no white in the room; the colors ranged from black and deep plum to honey beige. It was an atmosphere that encouraged heavy-liddedness: sensuality or sleep.

As I returned to my chair next to Elizabeth's bed, I stopped to run my fingers over the carving on the drawer of a dresser, a pattern that resembled fabric billowing in a wind. The designer had been an extravagant person, I thought, a southern European protesting displacement to the plains and the long winters of the American Midwest.

"You're to cosset *me*, not my furniture," Elizabeth said.

I thought, *I have a cosseting touch.* I went to Elizabeth and rested my hands on her shoulders. She smiled questioningly. With the thumb and forefinger of each hand, I grasped the muscles at the juncture of her neck and shoulders.

Elizabeth gasped and said, "You're surprisingly strong."

"But not dangerously so. I know my strength."

"But you may not know my weakness."

How weak was Elizabeth? It was difficult to learn the physical and emotional frailties of a new companion. Old people are likely to exaggerate and display their weaknesses and to hide their strengths. I always assumed my companions were stronger than they seemed.

I kneaded Elizabeth's neck muscles slowly but firmly for two or three minutes. I could feel her relax. She continued to smile, and we looked into each other's eyes. I couldn't tell whether I was smiling or not. I thought I had better stop.

As I stepped back and sat down next to her, Elizabeth said, "That was pleasureful. It's been some time since my body has given me anything but pain or anxiety."

I thought, *Some people confuse those things— pleasure, pain, and anxiety. My kind of people.*

"Tell me about your day," Elizabeth said.

"It was spiritual. Or spiritualist. I attended a church service and a séance."

"Which did you prefer?"

"The séance, I suppose. No one was pretending to be virtuous there."

"But we have to pretend to be virtuous, Jillian."

"But no one *is* virtuous."

"No. But we have to pretend, my dear. That's all that keeps us from killing one another."

It was time to change the subject. "Let me read to you," I said.

"Yes. I suppose that's always preferable to reality."

"I could read some nonfiction. A travel book, if you have one."

"I *don't* have one . . . wouldn't have one. I don't respect anyone who has to substitute observation for imagination. My idea of a travel book is the one about Gulliver."

I couldn't discuss literature with Elizabeth. The only literary opinion I had was the obvious one that people seem to need stories, whether in books, movies, or plays. But I had no idea why that was true.

I took a book at random from the bookcase: *Ballads of the British Isles*. Like all of the volumes in Elizabeth's collection, it was old. I opened it to a marked place and, squinting in the lamplight, began to read a long poem with the odd title "The Lady Turned Serving Man":

> You beauteous ladies great and small,
> I write unto you one and all,
> Whereby that you may understand
> What I have suffered in this land.

The ballad described how a young woman, after her husband is killed by thieves, changes her name "From fair Elise to Sweet William," cuts her hair, dresses in man's clothing, and becomes a "serving man." The author made no attempt to explain why fair Elise would want to do such a thing.

As I read, Elizabeth listened carefully and solemnly and didn't seem to think, as I did, that the ballad was silly, even when we got to the line, "Sweet William was a lady gay." Elise/William becomes a servant to the king, and after her identity is revealed, "He [the king] took Sweet William for his wife." The last two lines were: "The like before was never seen,/A serving man to be a queen." Even that didn't make Elizabeth smile. She merely looked wistful and asked me to read the ballad to her again.

After I repeated the lines, we sat in silence. I thought about what I had just read. Folk ballads were supposed to deal with basic human concerns and emotions, weren't they? Was there a feminist message in the poem? Did every woman want to become a man at least for a time?

I said to Elizabeth, "You're fond of that poem."

"You're not?"

"No. I don't understand it. What's the point?"

"Just change, I suppose. The will to change ... metamorphosis. Could any change be more dramatic than a change of sex?"

"Only one that I can think of."

"Yes?"

"Death."

Elizabeth looked amused but not enough to smile. She said, "Do you think, Jillian, that you're more interested in death than in sex?"

I hesitated, but then said, "Yes."

"We're agreed," Elizabeth said. "The sex act is an act of vanity, as are all other acts except the act of death."

I didn't answer. As I had admitted, I was interested in death, but I wasn't interested in philosophizing about it. And I suspected there had been a time when Elizabeth's values had been less morbid, judging from the large pink-glassed mirror that faced the bed. I looked at her reflection. The mirror transformed her into a young woman. Her hair appeared to be pale blond rather than white, and the hollows and seams of her face were blurred. Had she been the one who placed the mirror where it would reflect the activities of her and her bedmate? The placement indicated either vanity or voluptuousness.

I looked at Elizabeth's reflection more carefully and realized that in middle age she had been beautiful. When she had spoken to me about the disadvantages of beauty, she had spoken to me from personal experience. The mirror, I thought, might have been intended not to add piquancy to acts of love but to give one of the participants an admired prospect to help pass the time. And why was the mirror still there? Did Elizabeth still see herself as attractive, or did she enjoy watching the disintegration of her beauty?

Elizabeth, seeing me staring, answered my unspoken question. "I had forgotten about that mirror. Shall I have it taken down?"

"No. It might mean bad luck."

"I'm prepared for bad luck, my dear. I have flourished on it for years."

"Am I part of your bad luck? Is that why I'm here?"

"No. I rather think you are here to supply an ending to my bad luck—an absolute ending."

Before I could reply, Elizabeth said, "Go now. I'll rest."

As I stood up to leave, I watched my reflection. I didn't think I looked like someone who knew anything about absolute endings. I looked like someone with a cosseting touch.

14 | *Jack and Jill*

Soon after I left Elizabeth's room, there was a telephone call from John Ellis, who said he would arrive at the front door of the Dobb house in an hour and would expect me either to invite him in or to go out for a drive with him. It was the first time I had heard him issue an ultimatum, and I was surprised at his vehemence. Even so, I suspected that if I just ignored him he wouldn't have the courage to force the issue.

John, like his late mother, was a person who was confused by the uses of authority. His mother's confusion had led her to seclusion and timidity. John tried to come to terms with his confusion by taking on a role of ill-respected but total authority: He became a baseball umpire. John, who wanted to be liked by everyone, managed only to become respected by almost everyone. But no one *likes* an umpire. Players are not encouraged to, or wouldn't want to, fraternize with umpires. John became as solitary as his mother, although not exactly in a secluded setting.

John and his mother had both needed my companionship. Apparently, John still needed it. When he walked up the steps at six o'clock, I opened the door and stepped out into the shadows of the long, graceful, pillared porch. I stepped close to John and raised my face in what I was afraid might be a too blatant invitation. John looked at me sternly, said, "Oh shit," and kissed me delicately.

As we drove to a country-inn restaurant we had visited some months before, I let John babble nervously—and uncharacteristically—about the elaborate efforts he had made to find me before running into us at the roadhouse.

"For a while I was lucky," he said. "I thought I should get serious about becoming a private investigator."

Heroic and toughly romantic. Philip Marlowe. When he saw me on the porch of the Dobb house, he was seeing Lauren Bacall. Not me, not reality, but an American dream.

"I asked around and found out you had taken a bus out of town. I went to the pharmacy where the bus stops. The clerk remembered you had taken the 9:12 A.M. I found the driver. He had twelve safety badges on his tie. How does he get it off and on? Does he have to take those badges off every night and put them on every morning? Anyway, he remembered your father's keyboard case. He thought at first it must have held rifles, but he didn't know what someone who was blind could do with rifles. He finally decided it must have been fishing rods. A blind man can fish. But he was relieved when I told him what it really was. The driver said you got off in Plaines. It wasn't hard to find the bar where you waited for the taxi."

I said, "I gather you picked up more than just information in the bar."

John couldn't suppress a little smile. I asked him if a private eye isn't supposed to know better than to sleep with bar girls. He grunted but still smiled. "Then," he said, "I did something I thought was very clever."

"But not clever enough."

"Not quite. I knew about how long you had waited for the taxi. I figured out how far it must have come, and I went to every town that distance away and asked people who drove for hire whether they had picked you up."

"And they all said no."

"Right. I figured one of them lied, but I didn't know which one."

"Now you know."

"Yes. Did you pay her to keep quiet?"

"No. But someone smarter than both of us might have."

The restaurant was unpretentious. It offered only a choice of steaks, prime ribs, or lake perch (brought in daily from Wisconsin), together with corn sticks, baked potato (without foil wrapping), field lettuce, home-grown hothouse tomatoes, apple pie, and homemade vanilla ice cream. No urine-ish spices from Thailand and no silly fruit from Australia.

While we waited for the food, John's private-eye persona began to drop away. His face was like an animated wood sculpture; his eyes and his long straight hair were the same walnut shade as his skin, which was still dark from this year's stint with the Boys of Summer. Beneath the solidity was the vulnerability he could never quite conceal. I asked him what he had been doing since his mother's death.

"Going through her letters and papers; working on the house."

The house was an authentic, turreted, carpenter-gothic masterpiece that, owing largely to John's devotion, had never been altered or neglected. He knew all the house's secrets: the colors of its successive coats of paint, the network of pipes and wires that spread through the darkness beneath its plaster. He, like his late mother, knew its quiet history: in which rooms his forebears had suppressed their anger or implied their love.

I said, "Do you still love the house?" I was afraid that after his mother's death his attitude might have changed.

"I couldn't stop."

John, I recalled, was someone who had trouble both starting and stopping his emotions.

"That house has been, except for baseball and you, everything to me."

"You forgot to include jazz."

"Except for that, too. How's your father doing?"

"He's all right. Trying to resist having a good time."

"Walter's is the place for that. Anyway, I knew you would show up there eventually."

"Your sleuthing instinct again?"

"It worked. It got me what I wanted."

John reached out and touched my hand—something he wouldn't have done in public a few weeks earlier. I didn't trust the gesture. I withdrew my hand and changed the subject. "You said you've been working on the house."

"Just little things. I built an oak container into the mantel shelf above the fireplace. For Mom's ashes."

Why was he telling me this? Was it true? Looking not at me but at the menu, he continued, "At night I would build a fire and sit in front of it with one of her boxes of letters. There were dozens of boxes, hundreds of letters. After reading one, I would flip it into the flames. I know Mom better now than I ever did when she was alive. It's as if she had a secret life."

The waiter arrived, and while we were ordering, I felt a little unpleasant emotion that I soon realized was jealousy. When I knew Mrs. Ellis, the people she had corresponded with had either died or had become too vague to reply. I hadn't known about the letters. Hundreds of them. Correspondence was apparently the one thing she had done to excess.

"What are the letters like?" I asked after the waiter left.

"It's hard to explain. They're not her letters, of course; they're the answers to her letters. It's like seeing a portrait of her, but seeing it in a distorting mirror."

John became silent again as the waiter brought our wine. He was apparently only uneasy about what the letters might have meant. I was sorry he had burned them. I thought I might have been able to find some meaning in them.

John was not one to brood, however. "When someone gets around to sorting *my* papers," he said, "they'll find mostly old telephone bills."

During the rest of the meal, things lightened up. John showed off by cutting his steak with his fork. He told me confusing anecdotes about the Midwest baseball league and less confusing stories about the history of jazz. Then, just before we left the restaurant, he handed me a note written in what I recognized as his mother's handwriting. "I didn't burn this one," John said. The note read:

Dearest Son:

If you value my memory, you will treat Jillian with understanding and affection.

Mother

I wasn't surprised when, on the way home, John pulled the car onto a side road and parked. I *was* surprised when he put his hands around my neck with his thumbs against my arteries. "Is this how it was?" he asked. What frightened me more than the pressure of his hands was the indecipherable expression on his face. I had no idea whether his action was a serious threat or a bad joke.

Then he lowered his hands along my body and began to take a more conventional action. As he unbuttoned my coat, a conscienceless part of me began to send out pleasure signals, but another part reminded me that I might be about to make a blackmail payment.

John proceeded with enthusiasm and an obvious

knowledge of his craft. I felt as if we were engaged in some specialized athletic contest whose rules I didn't understand.

"You prefer it this way, don't you?" I whispered.

"Which way, my sweet?"

"With impediments. The adolescent way."

"Mmm."

John wasn't hearing me. He was a hound on the scent. Clothes—both John's and mine—were opened, lowered, raised, discarded. Following the wordless directions of his grasp, I squirmed and shifted, allowing him to investigate and, I suppose, pay homage to my body with his lips, teeth, and tongue. John's eyes opened only briefly as he moved from one objective to another, but my gaze was steady and unblinking as he gradually revealed his body. The firmness and balance of his facial features seemed to disintegrate as he proceeded. The slight flabbiness of his waist and the hairiness of his body tempered his air of innocence. Sex diminishes us, I thought; each act takes us farther from youth.

And yet I was not totally displeased. My pleasure, however, was with myself. At one point, I adjusted the rearview mirror so that I could see my face. I thought of the large mirror facing Elizabeth's bed. My features, unlike John's, benefited from the contrast with my nakedness. The firmness and fullness of my body lent a dignity and reliability to my expression. Against my will, I told myself that few people of either sex could refuse to be my companion after seeing me nude. Vanity. The sex act, as Elizabeth had said, was an act of vanity.

John's vanity had begun to exceed mine. He was crouched above me, half kneeling, looking down and smiling triumphantly. He was not looking at me, though, but at his stiff, slightly swaying penis, as if he regretted having to lose sight of it. Eventually, he put it out of sight after a complex maneuver in which he donned a condom and brought us face to face in a sitting position, our hands on each other's shoulders. John was staring down at our laps as if counting pubic hairs. I put my fingers under his chin and raised his head so that he was looking at my face. He closed his eyes.

This was his version of the understanding and affection his mother had asked him to show me.

15 | *A Pact Renewed*

When I arrived home—I had begun to think of it that way—I was exhausted and disgruntled. Elizabeth, however, was alert and refreshed after her long sleep. She had just finished bathing, and her bathroom door was open, releasing moist, perfumed air into the bedroom. The thought of bathing enticed me, but I went to sit with Elizabeth immediately. That's what she wanted and deserved. If I expected her one day to accede to my wishes, I must now accede to hers.

"Have David and Eva left?" I asked.

Elizabeth hesitated. She had apparently put her children out of her mind already. "Yes. Hours ago." She peered at me. "You're disheveled," she said. "Have you had a sexual encounter?"

"Yes."

"I can smell it."

"I'm sorry."

"It's a pleasant smell. Or so I always thought. But *you* don't look pleased."

"No. I was taken advantage of after a fashion."

"Do you always feel that way about sex, that you're a victim?"

"No. Sometimes I feel that my partner is the victim."

Elizabeth smiled. She was wearing a lacy bedjacket over a pale blue nightdress. She had turned on the electric lights in the room. Her face looked vulnerable

101

now with the furrows and creases revealed. "Were you a victim as a young woman?" I asked.

"Not in the bedroom—this bedroom. Andrew, my husband, was passive here. Passive but not indifferent. He would lie here as I do now and require me to, as he termed it, massage him. Often I would sit where you do now, in a bedside chair. He would lie with his eyes shut. I have no notion of what was in his mind at those times."

The mirror at the foot of the bed must have been for Elizabeth, I thought.

"How unpleasant for you," I said.

"Not at all. I loved it. There are few things as majestic as the male member ejaculating . . . but you've probably had enough of that sort of thing for one day."

"Yes. Definitely. I'm still inquisitive about your marriage, though. I wouldn't have thought your husband was passive."

"Oh, he wasn't. Not outside the bedroom. He was—or wanted to be—one of the last of the robber barons . . . but he didn't have their cunning, or their charitable impulses or cultural aspirations. He mined things. He fouled the land, and he exploited many people, including himself."

"And including you?"

"No. I was inviolate. He didn't respect me, but he protected me . . . in the same way he protected all his other possessions. Although, after the twins were born, he grew less protective. He became unfaithful."

"He didn't like the twins?"

"Not at first. He got to like David, I believe. Andrew died young—not yet sixty—while David was undergoing some extreme, and late-arriving, forms of adolescent confusion. David's irresponsibility may have had something to do with Andrew's decline. In any case, his money became inaccessible to David—or to anyone else but me, for that matter. Most of his wealth consists of gold bars stacked in a cave in a small mountain he bought in Oregon. He was devoted to gold. 'People always tarnish,' he would say, 'but gold never does. Gold is good for the soul.'" Elizabeth turned to look at me. "Are you fond of gold, Jillian?"

"No. And my husband wasn't, either. He liked things that were tarnished—especially other women."

Elizabeth considered that statement for a moment and then decided she didn't want me to elaborate on it. She said instead, "You never had any children, I think you said. Be grateful."

"The twins don't seem so monstrous."

"You don't know them well."

"Eva said she and Shirley might come to live here."

Elizabeth's features moved around as if searching for an unattainable expression and finally settled into a look of mild annoyance. "It will be against my wishes, but I don't suppose that will stop her."

It occurred to me that I might be able to use Eva's decision to my advantage. I had begun to think that my situation in the Dobb household was too dangerous and that Father and I should move on once more, away from John Ellis and David Dobb. I said, "Perhaps you won't need a companion if Eva and Shirley come to live here. Maybe I should leave you."

Elizabeth reached out and took my hands. "Nonsense," she said. Her eyes had begun to blink rapidly, and she was biting the corner of her lower lip. "They would give me no companionship. They would take from me. You will give to me." Elizabeth's eyes were moist and seemed to reflect genuine affection. She looked quickly at my hair, my lips, my shoulders and breasts, and then into my eyes. "You'll stay, won't you?"

There was more passion in her expression than there had been in John's at any time during that night's lovemaking. He was devoted to me and perhaps obsessed by me, but there was an element in

103

Elizabeth's personality—a depth—that I needed and that John could not supply. "Yes," I said. "I'll stay as long as you need me."

Elizabeth gave a little grunt of satisfaction. "I'll need you to the end," she said.

I wondered who would decide when the end had come.

Elizabeth looked relieved and a little playful now. "Eva and Shirley have no souls," she whispered. "You haven't forgotten our bargain, have you?"

"I have a good memory," I said and smiled.

"Let me test your memory. Memorize this: right 57, left 37, right 52, left 25. Can you repeat it?"

I did.

"Don't forget it, dear. Now, let me show you something." Elizabeth, waving aside my effort to help her, got quickly out of bed and walked to a painting that hung on the wall facing the bed—an age-darkened oil portrait by a primitive, but probably professional, painter. Elizabeth pressed a button on the left side of the frame and swung it out on hinges that were hidden along the right side. Recessed in the wall was a safe with the knob of a combination lock in its center.

"Test your memory," Elizabeth said. I dialed, alternately right and left: 57, 37, 52, 25. I felt the slight click, like a pulse beat, as I dialed the last number. Elizabeth turned a handle next to the dial and opened the safe. A small light in the interior created a yellowish glow as it reflected off a random jumble of jewelry, coins, and small ingots.

"It's all gold, isn't it?" I asked.

"Of course. It's what souls are traditionally sold for."

I remembered how I had leaned over Mrs. Ellis's bed a few weeks earlier, golden rings glinting on my fingers. I wondered where her soul was now. And it occurred to me that each of my departed employers had left me at least one gold object. "Selling one's soul is a supernatural act, isn't it?" I asked.

"Does the idea of the supernatural offend you?"

"I'm not sure. Father assures me there is such a thing—much more of it than anyone admits—but he also assures me that we should ignore it. He says that the best kind of rationalist is the kind who simply tries to decrease the power of the supernatural.

Elizabeth looked amused. "Why not simply learn to use its power instead of trying to suppress it?"

"Because the people who have such powers are often evil and stupid. And that's destructive."

Elizabeth raised a hand and ran the backs of her fingers across my cheek. "The more rational among us can also be destructive . . . isn't that true, Jillian?"

I nodded and thought of David.

16 | *Romance*

"Doesn't your father get lonely, Jillian?"

It was almost noon, and Elizabeth and I were having our usual brunch downstairs in the breakfast room. Elizabeth had orange juice and gin (equal parts) and bran cereal. I had coffee and glazed doughnuts. The room was dazzlingly sunny. I thought, *The stronger the light, the more mundane the conversation.* But perhaps I was misinterpreting Elizabeth's interest in Father.

"No, I don't think Father is lonely. He enjoys his little discomforts, his penance. And he has his music . . . and Mrs. Tickle."

"Oh, yes. His landlady. But I was wondering whether you might like it if your father—Matthew—lived here with us. We certainly have enough room. And you would worry less about him."

I thought, *And maybe you would prefer his companionship to mine.* But I didn't want to sound petty and jealous. I said, "I really don't worry about him. And if Eva and Shirley come to live here, you might find it burdensome to have so many people around."

"Don't worry, my dear. You will protect me."

That would be a new role for me, and maybe an interesting one. "I'll mention your idea to Father," I said.

Elizabeth wasn't going to be put off with vague

promises, though. "Maybe you can ask Matthew to visit us tonight," she said.

So I picked up Father after dinner that night and guided him through the cool, dark streets to the Dobb house. Father was displeased. "Is this Dobb going to turn out to be an interfering bitch?" he asked. As always, he had the words that would please me.

When the three of us were settled around the fireplace with ice tinkling against the sides of our whiskey glasses, the possibility of Father living with us seemed less objectionable. For a few minutes, we found drinking preferable to talking. I noticed that as the level of liquid in a glass becomes lower, the pitch of its ice-cube tinkling became higher—which seemed illogical to me. It was something that Father would know about.

"Are the tinkles getting higher?" I asked.

"Sure," he said. "When you want to make a little xylophone from glasses, you fill them all up with water. Then you take a little out of the first one and a little more out of the next one and so on. I've seen people do it with whiskey—take eight full glasses and ping and sip until they had a diatonic scale. Then they could play bagpipe tunes."

Elizabeth suppressed a giggle and said, "Oh, Matthew."

I don't like giggles, and I don't like the name Matthew.

"Matthew," Elizabeth said, "was one of the four evangelists, wasn't he?" Her drink had started her on free association already.

"Yes, of course," Father said. "But that's not what my parents had in mind when they named me. My father was a photographer. I'm named for Matthew Brady."

I hadn't known that, and I resented his giving the information to a stranger before he gave it to me.

There was still so much I didn't know about Father. From my fifth through my thirtieth year, he had been out of my life and my mother's life. He had deserted us to join an evangelist's tent show. Years later, he became a part of my mother's life again only long enough to allow her to plunge two knitting needles simultaneously into his eyes as he slept. He refused to file criminal charges against her, saying that he only got what he deserved. I don't know where my mother is now, but I hope she is getting what *she* deserves.

"I didn't get to know much about photography," Father was saying, "but I found out a lot about evangelism in the days before TV replaced tents."

He was talking only to Elizabeth, who was looking at him in a way I had never seen her look at anyone or anything previously: uncritically, if not worshipfully.

"Tell me about faith healing," Elizabeth said to Father. "How much does faith have to do with it?"

"You mean, do the patients heal themselves with their faith?"

"Yes."

"Not my patients. Mine get a big jolt of hocus-pocus power."

"But you're not the source of the power," Elizabeth said.

"No. I'm like a lightning rod. I attract the jolt and pass it on."

There was a playful tone to Elizabeth's voice, but I knew she was not joking. "Where does the power come from?" she asked.

"There are different theories about that. I think it's best not to ask."

"There can't be too many theories, Matthew."

"Basically two, as far as I know."

"The Lord of Light or the Lord of Darkness," Elizabeth said.

"That's about it."

"Which do you think it is?"

"I told you, I don't ask." Father held out his hands to her. "You tell *me,*" he said.

Elizabeth looked at me as if asking my permission. There was no encouragement in the look I returned, and I didn't say anything. Elizabeth wasn't going to let me spoil her game, though. She rose—a little less stiffly than usual—and walked over to take Father's hands. He was to blame for the situation, of course. He had challenged Elizabeth, and she no longer received enough challenges to allow her to turn them down. She took Father's hands and made a faint squealing sound. He was being dishonest with her and using a technique he told me he had used in his professional years: he gave a brief, full-strength squeeze and followed it with a slight tug, which put the victim (as he called them) off balance. When he did it quickly enough, it created a disorienting sense of shock. Elizabeth lost her balance and fell forward slightly, putting her hands on Father's shoulders.

Father turned his head in my direction, and I was sure that if he had been capable of it, he would have winked. Then he said to Elizabeth, "Well, do you feel the power?"

"Yes, Matthew."

"And is it good or evil?"

"Both," Elizabeth said. She continued to lean forward over him with her arms straight and her hands on his shoulders. She shifted her weight several times and moved her feet apart. I thought she was trying to push herself up to a normal standing position, and I was about to help her, when it occurred to me that her movement was a more or less unconscious reaction.

When the doorbell rang, I was grateful for the distraction. No one wants to watch a geriatric romance develop, especially if it involves one's own parent.

The person who had rung the doorbell was John Ellis. He was holding a large bunch of bronze and gold chrysanthemums, and his expression was as soulful as Elizabeth's. "I wanted to apologize for last night," he said. I suspected what he really meant was that he was ready for a repeat performance. But I thought he and Elizabeth might as well meet.

I asked John in and made the introduction. He was wearing a baseball cap as usual, and when he took it off, it left a horizontal line across the hair at the back of his head. He was more interested in renewing his acquaintance with Father than with getting to know Elizabeth. John and Father shared an interest in jazz and had spent many evenings together when I was Mrs. Ellis's companion. John was fond enough of Father to be willing to appear in public with him and to endure the deluge of bad jokes that his friends came up with when they saw him with a blind man. Umpires have enough clumsy humor directed at them without encouraging it.

Elizabeth seemed more interested in John Ellis than I had expected her to be. They started an intense little conversation, and I assumed it was based on the fact that John's mother had been my former employer.

"Your mother was fortunate to have had Jillian as a companion," Elizabeth said to John.

"Yes. Mother was fond of Jillian."

"Did she love her, do you think?"

John, understandably, looked surprised. "Up to a point," he said.

"I thought love was an unrestrained feeling," Elizabeth said. "Can you love someone only up to a point?"

"I was thinking of the point of death."

Elizabeth looked at John with increased respect. "You're not a truly romantic person, then. You don't think love transcends the grave."

"Maybe for the person who's standing at the side of the grave. But not for the person who's in it."

"In any case," I said to John, "your mother is not in

a grave." I turned to Elizabeth. "John's mother was cremated. Her ashes are on his fireplace."

"In his fireplace?"

"*On,* not in . . . on the mantel," John said.

I wondered how this simple introduction had turned so quickly into a discussion of death. It was, I supposed, a result of my influence, part of my mission. The topic that most people avoid at all costs was introduced naturally in my presence. I was pleased. Death and romance. I was beginning to feel a stimulation I had not experienced in my encounter with John the night before. I looked around our little group. All of us were stimulated, I sensed, in a way that belied our years. There was an adolescent intensity in the room.

Father tried to break the spell. He knew more about emotional highs than the rest of us, and he mistrusted them. He asked John about the minor-league baseball season that had just ended—a season that Father had followed by occasionally listening to radio broadcasts of games. Father wanted a detailed description of a certain pitcher—a middle-aged, out-of-condition castoff from the major leagues who had had a remarkably successful season, winning through cleverness and the force of his eccentric personality rather than through ability. Father and John were starting a process I had heard many times before. If no one interrupted them, they would drift back and forth between two topics: baseball and jazz. According to Father, jazz musicians have always tended to like baseball, although few baseball players like jazz. According to John, most baseball players don't like *anything,* including baseball.

Elizabeth and I didn't take part in John and Father's conversation, and we didn't start one of our own. The talk was continuous but not enthusiastic. John glanced often at me; Father tilted his head toward Elizabeth in the peculiar little gesture that was his version of a glance. Names were evoked: the pitcher Bobo Newsom, the saxophonist Sonny Stitt, and one of my father's favorites, the baseball player who became an evangelist, Billy Sunday. But soon the conversational energy wavered under the weight of unspoken topics, and John turned to me and suggested that we leave.

Before we reached his car, John had placed his hand on my waist and had maneuvered his fingers under my jacket and sweater, exposing a little patch of my skin to air that was cold enough to have formed a dusting of frost on the top of the car. I was pleased, but what pleased me was the chill and not John's little gesture.

"A woman doesn't like to have attention called to her waist," I said. "Waists are never as taut or slender as they should be."

"What *does* she like to have attention drawn to?"

"Her soul, John."

John allowed some little lines of puzzlement to appear on his forehead under the visor of his baseball cap. He wasn't sure whether he should laugh. "The soul is a little difficult to put your finger on."

"Yes, It's not simply a matter of pulling a sweater up. But if you expect to keep visiting me, you'll have to touch more than my body."

"That's partly what I wanted to talk to you about," John said. We got into the car, and he turned on the heater and let the engine idle, the twentieth-century equivalent of sitting before a cozy fire. John looked comfortable and pleased with the arrangement, but I've never been comfortable in automobiles. Father, partly as a result of growing up in Detroit, never liked cars. He says the mass production of private passenger cars destroyed the family and society—first in America and then everywhere else in the First and Second Worlds. The automobile allowed people—mostly white people—to abandon the cities and flee to the suburbs. It cut us all adrift; it made moderately intelligent people feel godlike, and it made stupid people feel machinelike. According to Father, it took our humanity away. My own reasons for disliking cars are less elaborate: first, I lost my virginity in one; second, I'm terrified of driving in dense, fast-moving traffic; and third, it's more difficult for someone to trace you if you don't own or rent an automobile.

But John had traced me—or found me—and I had to know what he planned to do. He looked benign and respectful. "I've taken a room at Walter's," he said.

"At Walter's? At Walpurgis?"

"Yes."

"I thought they rented their rooms by the hour."

"They make exceptions. And it's the closest thing they have to a hotel near Serena."

"There would also be companionship available."

"I want your companionship."

I remembered Father saying that a companion is just a type of hooker. "I'm not sure I know what you want from me, John."

"I want several things," John said. "For one, I want to know if you're an evil person."

"No. Not according to my definition of evil. But I suppose your definition might differ from mine."

John accepted the implied challenge. "In your definition," he asked, "is a murderer an evil person?"

"What does that have to do with me?"

John peered at me intently through the darkness. His eyes had the perceptive intensity of a hawk's, but not the fierceness. "Well, tell me this," he said. He hesitated and lowered his voice. He turned his eyes away as he spoke. "Did you kill my mother?"

I didn't hesitate. I looked toward him steadily, and I touched his hand. "No. I wouldn't put it that way."

"How would you put it?"

"I'd say I was involved in her death."

John considered my statement. "Would you say your involvement was active?"

"Yes. But the action involved was one of love. You may not understand that."

"I understand that," John said. "That's why I'm going to ask you this question: Will you marry me?"

"No, John. Of course not." I was elated. Love—not my love, of course—had conquered all.

When, in an hour or so, we picked up Father and took him home, he couldn't stop smiling. At first, he refused to explain his delight. But as I was leaving him, he said, "Elizabeth gave me a massage."

17 | *Idyll and Influx*

The rest of that night was idyllic. It was the last night Elizabeth and I were to spend alone in that house together, the last night I would experience a particular type of friendship and peace.

I ran a hot bath for Elizabeth. Steamy moisture filled the large, cool bathroom. Mist rose as in a Hollywood fantasy—we could have been in an anteroom in heaven or hell.

I helped Elizabeth into the tub and soaped her back. "It pleased me to bathe the twins when they were infants," she said. "I have always thought of them as emissaries of the supernatural, and for a few months I thought they were a benevolent force. I actually examined the area around their shoulder blades for signs of incipient wings."

I ran my fingers lightly over Elizabeth's upper back.

"No angel I," she said. "All you'll find there are signs of poor posture." I traced her shoulder blades lightly with the tips of my fingers. "I must have been obsessed with wings. There was a book that my father owned. What could it have been? It was illustrated with engravings, many of them depicting angels. I had forgotten, but when my breasts began to appear, I prayed—literally—that I would grow wings instead. I would stand with my back to the large mirror and look over my shoulder with a hand mirror. As you can see, my breasts did arrive. They were a disappointment, but at least they were small disappointments . . .

perhaps as the result of prayer. Small breasts are a blessing. In your youth, they prevent the cruder boys from being attracted to you, and when you're the age I am now, they're less—a bit less—hideous."

Elizabeth straightened her posture and pulled back her shoulders. She placed her hands at her collar bones and pressed the flesh upward, raising and rounding her breasts. I was sure she was thinking about my father.

After Elizabeth was in bed, I bathed myself quickly, thinking not of my body but my soul. Then I went to Elizabeth's bedside and read aloud to her a passage she had requested from Charlotte Brontë's *Jane Eyre,* the passage in which Mr. Rochester dresses as a gypsy woman and tells Jane's fortune, making her kneel before him and telling her that her destiny is shown not in her palm but in her face.

When I had finished reading the passage, I remembered that the ballad I had read to Elizabeth recently had also described someone who had pretended to be of the opposite sex. I suspected that the similarity was not a coincidence, but I decided not to ask Elizabeth about it. Instead, she was the one to ask a question. "Is *Jane Eyre* a true portrait of love, Jillian? I thought you might have an understanding of that."

"I don't think I understand love," I said. "But maybe that's where true love exists—in books. I've read *Jane Eyre* aloud to another companion, and it didn't seem to me that it had anything to do with the real world. Charlotte Brontë might have fooled us by taking things that really can exist, like blindness and houses that burn down, and combining them with things that don't exist, like love. I don't know. Father might know, but I doubt if he would admit it."

Elizabeth looked reticent for the first time since I

had known her. "Would you permit me to love your father, Jillian?"

"Yes. But I won't permit him to love you, Elizabeth."

"I don't require that."

I wondered if there were something about the Dobb house that initiated odd romantic impulses. Was it possible for a house to haunt people? To lead them to excessive affections? I thought I had heard of such things—a convent, was it, that led nuns to abandon their piety and discipline? I wondered if the various people who were about to come to live in the house were wise.

Late the next morning, when I went downstairs to prepare Elizabeth's breakfast tray, I found Eva and Shirley seated at the kitchen table. A large assemblage of luggage, trunks, and boxes filled one corner of the room. Standing in back of Shirley, with a hand on her shoulder, was Charlie Blake, the young piano player. The three of them smiled at me. Then I noticed that there was yet another person in the room. Standing unobtrusively next to Charlie Blake was a type of person I had never expected to see in the Dobb house: a young child, a boy. I supposed his age was somewhere between three and seven, but because of my limited experience with (and interest in) children, my guess had to be vague.

The overall impression I got of the little group was of youth and guilt. Eva, her eyes glittering and the skin blotched pink across her cheekbones, looked like a hyperactive child who had been caught doing something forbidden. "Good morning, Jillian," she said. "We've arrived. Charlie Blake helped us move. You remember him from Walter's." Then she moved to put her hand on the boy's head. "This is Gus," she said. "Charlie's son."

Gus smiled at me shyly, and I felt the inevitable impulse of protectiveness and tenderness. It was an impulse I always resisted. I suspected that the smile didn't indicate friendliness but was a mannerism that the child had developed out of a sense of self-promotion. Although my avoidance of children was more a matter of indifference than of dislike, I could usually find grounds for disapproval in my encounters with young people. Mostly I objected to their self-obsession. They always expect the adult, of whom they are oblivious, to walk around them.

I wouldn't have been a good mother. It also may be that one's ability to love or even to tolerate children diminishes with age. Elizabeth, for example, seemed to have contradictory memories of her experience in raising the twins. We become disillusioned, and we transfer our accumulated distrust of adults to our children; in most cases, it seems justified to me. The quality I found most attractive in children was their taste for the irrational and the frightening. In that sense, they seem closer to reality than their parents do. But generally, I feel about people under thirty-five the way the hippies of the 1960s felt about people over twenty-five: they're not to be trusted.

I looked at Shirley and Charlie, who were not trying very hard to be adults, and at Eva, who probably thought she had been one too long. None of them had the reassuring presence of Elizabeth or Father, who (as they had recently demonstrated) were capable of silliness but knew the implications of their behavior. They might distress their friends, but not inadvertently.

Shirley and Eva were currently at the mercy of some hormones that could make victims of them or of anyone around them. Charlie had a look of extreme vulnerability. His approach to the world was that of someone at a party who is trying to be polite but is also trying to listen to another conversation. In his case, I suspected, it was some internal melody he was listening to.

There was an awkward pause. The visitors were all wearing heavy down jackets, and the exertions of moving their luggage, combined with nervousness, had created a faint but unmistakable aroma of perspiration. Charlie looked down at his son. "His name's actually Gustav. His mother liked Mahler's music."

There was another pause. Then I said, "It could have been worse. She could have liked Mozart."

Eva smiled, Shirley looked indifferent, and Charlie looked puzzled. Little Gustav asked, "Wolfgang or Leopold?" I decided Gus was older than I had guessed.

Eva said, with an odd animation, "Gus lives with his mother, who is studying to be a concert harpist."

I remembered that Elizabeth had told me Eva's *ex*-husband was a concert pianist. Musicians are not good spouses, I thought. Most people are bad spouses, but musicians are worse than most. My husband, whom I tried never to think of, had been—to my present amazement—a jazz drummer.

"I'll tell Elizabeth you're here," I said.

Elizabeth accepted my announcement cautiously. "Tell them I won't alter my activities . . . we won't alter our activities . . . for them. They must adapt to us. Have them see the housekeeper about rooms, linens, and meals. What do we call the housekeeper?"

"Mary. Mary Hess."

"Tell Mary we will increase the food budget and her salary as required."

Elizabeth's tone was stern, but she didn't seem distressed. "I think you're not displeased," I said.

She ignored my suggestion. "Does that young pianist plan to live here?"

"They didn't say. But I doubt it. He just helped them move their things, I think."

"The spare bedroom in this wing must stay vacant. Tell Mary that."

The house had a good supply of bedrooms. There were three—including mine—in Elizabeth's wing of the second floor. There were three more in another wing of the second floor, and there were two—former servants' quarters—on the floor above. I was grateful that Elizabeth wanted to isolate us from the others. Or, I wondered, did she plan to put someone else in the unoccupied room adjoining hers? She didn't allow me much time for speculation. "I was hoping, as you know, that your father might consider taking that room. You'd like that, wouldn't you?"

"I'm not sure. But it's *his* preference we have to consider."

"Of course, my dear. Perhaps you'd like to visit him this afternoon and ask him what his preference is."

From downstairs, I heard the laughter of a child.

There was an unaccustomed sense of life in the Dobb house.

I was uneasy.

18 | *Soul Talk*

As I walked to Father's rooming house that afternoon, I felt an unusual sense of vulnerability and melancholy. The wind was cold and gusty, and the sky was an undifferentiated gray. There was no indication of what part of the sky the sun was in. The trees were skeletal; their bright leaves had been collected and burned. In front of a restfully severe gray house, free of the gothic tracery of the Dobb house, there was a clump of orange-scarlet bittersweet. It was beautiful, and it named my mood. I had been uneasy when I went out, but there was also a spot of pleasure in my mood, like the spot of color in front of the gray house.

It was unusual for me to be anything but confident and sure of my goals and beliefs, but when I got to Father's room, I was compelled to ask him an unusual question even before I sat down or before he could leave his keyboard. "Is there such a thing as the soul, Father?"

"Does *my* daughter have to ask that? Didn't I explain that to you when you still hadn't figured out the potty?"

"Not just soul as in music and food, but *the* soul, as in religion."

"Yes, baby. There is such a thing."

"Can souls be bought and sold?"

"Somebody has scared Jillian," Father said. "It wasn't that preacher the other day, was it?" He

121

switched the speakers of his keyboard on and, accompanying himself with full, Debussyish chords, sang a little blues chorus:

Come here, pretty baby,
Sit down on your daddy's knee.
Come here, pretty baby,
Sit down on your daddy's knee.
Won't no one buy your soul
Long as you still got me.

I didn't sit on my daddy's knee, but I did sit on the sofa and listen to his thoughts about the soul. He stayed at his keyboard, turned the volume down, and punctuated his words with fragments from a jazz standard called "Sermonette."

"What do we know about the soul? It's immortal, they say, but I doubt that it is . . . (chord).

"The evidence is that only a few people have one . . . (chord).

"What pisses people off is that it's not necessarily the *good* people that have one . . . (chord).

"If you've got one, you've got the answer and you've got a goal. People are going to love you or hate you. They'll want to share it—to be your soulmate—or they'll want to take it away. When a soul is dark, like yours, people usually want to take it away."

I wondered whether Father knew how truly dark my soul was and what my goal was. He was using a mock-serious tone, and he seemed to be improvising his words the way he improvised his music. But he had obviously given the subject some thought, and there was a certain truth in what he said. Many people—often intelligent, privileged people—seem to lack a primary connection to life; they may have good manners, but in a more profound sense they don't know how to behave or what to do.

I've always known what to do.

And though you may question my judgment, I doubt if you could fail to admire my dedication.

With a big tremolo major chord, Father ended the tune he was playing. He said, "Are you really worried about those people?"

"I'm not sure."

"Not about Elizabeth, I hope."

"She says she wants to buy my soul . . . with gold."

"That's just her way of saying she loves you. The one to fear is the male-ish twin—David."

"Male-ish?"

"Everything about him is centerless; he needs a soul."

"Elizabeth wants you to come and live with us. Her daughter and granddaughter moved in this morning. There's too much ferment. David will probably move in, too. I need reinforcements. Or should I—we—retreat?"

"What the hell, sweetie, let's do a little combat. I'll join you."

"You're attracted to Elizabeth, aren't you? She's seventy-five years old, you know. Fifteen years older than you are."

"I'm blind, for Christ's sake. My priorities are different. I don't ask much—a good voice, good hands."

I was trying to think of a reply that wouldn't reveal the jealousy I was feeling. Father spoke first. "Her voice is like yours. A fancy contralto, formal and sexy. Her hands are like yours, too—good, slender bones, not fleshy. I'm not thrilled by plump hands. A little plumpness elsewhere doesn't hurt."

Father was merely flattering me, I knew, but that's what I wanted.

For although my dark soul was the source of most of my strength, my life had taken on stability only when I brought my soul into contact with souls that were sunnier or more rakish than mine.

123

I thought of my former employer-companions. Had I released their souls? And if so, to what pleasure or pain had I released them? I longed for those simpler times, when it was easier for me to have faith in my actions.

"What's John Ellis up to?" Father asked. "Was it just an accident that we ran into him?"

"Not exactly. He had been looking for us. I thought at first he wanted to cause trouble for us. But now he wants to marry me."

"As we both know," Father said, "marriage and trouble aren't necessarily different things."

"Yes. I suppose marriages are often acts of revenge."

"Whatever the reasons, we're a popular couple."

"They sense our happiness, and they want to share it."

"So, are you going to take John up on his offer?" Father was speaking too forcefully, trying to sound as if he thought the marriage was an alternative that might be worth considering.

"You know I wouldn't do that."

"John's got some good instincts."

"What you mean by that is that he likes jazz. But I don't think that's as much of a virtue as you do. His world isn't ours. If we were to have a rainstorm today, he would see it as an opportunity to practice his judgment. Would he let the teams play through it? Would there be delays? Or would he call the game?"

"And what would *we* do if it rained today?"

"We would both feel better about the world. You like weather you can hear, and I like weather that makes people want to huddle together, that reminds us of uncontrollable forces."

"You should have more sympathy for the people who make their livings in tents and stadiums, sweetie."

"Sympathy is exactly what I have. But not love."

"So John's out of luck?"

"No. John's idea of luck is what the comedians call getting lucky. He'll get lucky—maybe with Eva, but if not, there's always Walpurgis."

"What?"

"Walter's. 'Walpurgis' is what their sign says."

"I didn't know that," Father said. He took his glasses off and rubbed the bridge of his nose. The glasses were his mask, and when he was without them, his mysterious attractiveness and his breezy self-confidence were diminished. I realized that the evangelists had destroyed his faith and that a faithless person was a hollow person.

Perhaps my faith and my soul were interchangeable. I gained a purity from my vocation as a companion. Mrs. Dobb would not—as she had said—be trading her life for my soul. Instead, her life would nourish my soul and would give me the strength and faith to find yet another companion.

I looked at Father, a maimed and helpless man. Was I really, as I hoped, making him happy? Maybe in suggesting another way of life for me, he was asking for his own freedom.

There was a knock on the door. Father put his glasses back on. "Yes?" he said.

"Tea time," a woman's voice said, and the door opened. It was Mrs. Tickle. She didn't seem surprised to find me in the room; she had probably seen me arrive. There were three cups on the tea tray.

Mrs. Tickle looked more formidable than ever. She was not just physically imposing, but apparently emotionally invulnerable. I was going to test that invulnerability. After saying hello, I said, "I'm afraid my father will be moving out tomorrow, Mrs. Tickle."

She pulled her lower lip between her teeth for a moment but said simply, "That's short notice. I require a week's notice."

"We'll pay you an extra week's rent," I said.

"That's fair," she said. "All I want is to be treated fairly."

But I wondered if that were all Mrs. Tickle wanted. I wondered if she wanted to be treated affectionately. She and Father made one of those unexpectedly complementary couples. His ready-for-a-party informality was balanced by her hide-your-passion formality. Perhaps they could be happy indulging each other's excesses.

Father might learn to be happier sharing such a woman's life than he had been sharing mine. I looked at him and tried to see signs of disappointment in his expression. But it is hard to detect regret in an eyeless person. He said, "I'm just a rollin' stone, Mrs. T."

"Ja, ja," said Mrs. Tickle, echoing the character who loses her lover in *Rosenkavalier*. She glanced at me and turned to leave the room. I wasn't sure what emotion was behind the glance, but I knew it wasn't fondness.

I said, "I'll leave the key and the money on the bureau." She had closed the door behind her before I finished speaking.

Father played a bluesy little figure on his keyboard and sang, in his country-boy voice, a parody of the Muddy Waters song "Rollin' Stone":

> *Oh well, your mama said to me*
> *Just before you was born:*
> *Gonna have me a girl child*
> *And she's gonna have a restless soul.*

It wasn't my fault that Mrs. Tickle and Father liked different kinds of music.

19 | *One Man's Normality*

John Ellis—who wore a chest protector on his job and who had recently moved into a brothel—wanted to introduce me to the normal life. He was waiting in his car outside the rooming house when Father and I left.

"They told me you were here," he said. "Can I give you a lift? I thought it might help, what with the rain."

I watched John carefully as he put Father's luggage in the trunk of the car. John's persistent attention was forcing me to reassess him and to wonder whether I had underestimated him. As usual, he was wearing a baseball cap and warm-up jacket. The strength of his upper body was evident from the ease with which he lifted the heavy luggage. But his strength was offset by a slight lack of coordination.

The same traits, as I had been reminded recently, were evident in his lovemaking. He had remarkable vigor and stamina, but there was always some awkwardness at crucial moments that distracted me and kept me from experiencing as much pleasure as I might have. But as we drove the few blocks to the Dobb house, it occurred to me that my level of sexual desire in general had never been intense. I liked the idea of sex and had never avoided it, but the pleasure I derived from it was mild. I enjoyed the disrobing, the nudity, the seeing and being seen; I enjoyed the touching with hands and mouth; I could experience delicate orgasms from these events. But the penetration and sweaty athletics that followed were less interesting to me. My husband said my sexual nature had never developed beyond the childish phase of playing house. Perhaps he was right. He also pointed out, less kindly, and I think less accurately, that the sexual games that I preferred could be played as well with a woman as with a man.

John carried the luggage to Father's room, which connected with Elizabeth's through a door on the east wall of her room as mine did on the west. It occurred to me that Elizabeth had literally placed herself between me and Father. But I felt no resentment, only pleasure and anticipation of interesting developments.

When he had finished playing porter, John followed me into my bedroom and asked me to go out to dinner with him.

"You don't understand, John," I said. "My time belongs to Mrs. Dobb. Except on my day off, I can see you only with her permission. And I'm not going to bother her with constant requests. You'll have to find some other way of dealing with your randiness."

"That's not fair. That's not what it's about."

"What *is* it about, John?"

"Love. I love you. I want you to marry me and live a normal life. Have some children. There's still time for that."

The word *children* caused a twinge of some kind in my chest. Did he mean these things? If so, I should be less harsh with him.

"I have to see you more than once a week," John said.

"I'll find out what I can arrange. But you must leave now. I have to get Father settled. I'll call you."

John gave me his phone number and left. I sat down and thought about the situation. I would have to use caution in dealing with John. I wanted to be in his good graces but not necessarily in his bed. But I was in some moderate way both flattered and aroused by his attention. If John's desires were all I had to deal with, I probably would manage easily, as I had managed when his mother was alive. But now I had to accommodate myself to much more than that.

There were too many people in my life. The simplicity and sense of purpose that had taken me so many years to achieve were endangered. Perhaps it was as Father had said. People recognized my special qualities—my serenity—and they wanted to share them. John saw me as having something more important than his other interests; he knew that baseball is ultimately just a game and that even music is irrelevant to life and death.

I heard John's laughter from downstairs—a laughter as raggedly distinctive as his voice; a result, he said, of calling balls and strikes. He was one of those umpires who bellow their calls. The players are more likely to accept your call if you sound as if you have no doubt about it, he said.

I went to the head of the stairs. Cigarette smoke drifted up from the parlor, and I could indistinctly hear John speaking. He seemed to be talking about a house. I walked hesitantly down to the landing.

I heard Eva say, "Pear wood?"

"That's what I'm told. Its smooth grain makes it easier to carve intricate detail on. There are seven big panels—each one showing a deadly sin."

John was describing the study in his house, which I had seen many times from many vantage points, including the floor, while committing at least one of the sins.

"I *must* see it," Eva said.

I squatted so that I could see into the parlor.

"Anytime," said John. "I'm sure you'll like it." He reached out and touched Eva's hand; not as spontaneously as he pretended, I thought. He didn't look like a spurned suitor.

John had taken some photographs out of his wallet.

They were obviously pictures of his house—pictures he had never shown me. Of course, I had lived in the house and had not found it particularly interesting. Eva, however, was cooing with interest in either the house or John. "It's almost ecclesiastical," she said. "True gothic—the pinnacles and the tracery. Is that stained glass in the tall window?"

"Yes. There's more. A little round one here."

"A rose window."

"I guess."

"The ornamentation is in excellent condition."

"I've replaced a lot of it. I've got a scroll saw in the workroom, an antique that works on a treadle."

Eva erupted in a little litany of terms like *crenellation, batten,* and *pedimented gables.* I stood up and left the new friends to their enthusiasms. As I was leaving, Eva quoted an architect named Downing, who said that when tasteful homes emerge, it's evidence that order and culture have been established. As I went back up the stairs, I wondered whether it was that simple. I knew that there had been saints and artists whose homes hadn't been so tasteful. And I knew that many people who took great pride in their homes should have shown more concern for their values and beliefs.

Among the boxes that Eva brought, I had seen a series of large photo albums. I assumed they contained pictures of buildings she had designed as well as snapshots of her and her family. Someday when she was out of the house, I would look through the albums, and I was sure that even though I disliked her buildings, I would find more "order and culture" in them than in the images of her family.

When I returned to Elizabeth's room, she and Father were standing in the center of the floor, hand in hand. Elizabeth looked stronger and healthier than I had ever seen her look. She held out her free hand to me. I took it, apparently more firmly than I realized. "Gently, my dear," she said. There was a look of discomfort on her face. She was still frail and vulnerable after all.

I felt comfortable for the first time since I had left the house in the afternoon.

20 | *Metamorphosis*

It was after midnight before the house became silent and Elizabeth and I were able to relax and talk. Earlier in the evening I had sat in a corner of Elizabeth's room as she napped fitfully, tossing and murmuring. She spoke words I had never heard her speak before.

When she awakened fully, she threw the blankets aside and raised herself unsteadily to her feet. I moved quickly to take her arm, but she waved me aside. She went to her closet and brought out two robes I had never seen before. She threw one across the bed and put the other on. The one she wore looked as ridiculous on her as anything I could imagine. It was a floor-length housecoat of pink cotton with lace trim. Handwritten in three places on the robe was the crudely inked inscription "Bill Haley 4-Ever."

Elizabeth stood before her bureau mirror and looked at herself intently. She twirled awkwardly and hummed quietly. Then she steadied herself by placing her hands on the bureau. She moved her face close enough to the mirror so that her breath fogged the glass slightly. Her humming gradually became louder, and then she began to chant, haltingly and tunelessly, the inane words of "Rock Around the Clock."

I watched in embarrassed fascination. Elizabeth's actions had the quality of a ritual—something she had done many times before. But what did it mean to her? The robe could not have been hers. It was the garment of someone who was an adolescent or preadolescent in the late 1950s—someone who was more frivolous than Elizabeth had ever been.

When she had finished chanting the chorus, Elizabeth backed away from the mirror. Twirling once more, she threw the robe off and picked up the one that lay on the bed. The new one was an ordinary but elegant man's dressing gown made of maroon paisleyed silk. Elizabeth's movements grew more masculine but in a way more sensuous. She looked at me for the first time since her little show had begun. She took my right hand in her left and moved her right hand around my waist and rested it on the small of my back. Then I realized she expected me to dance with her. She began to sing again, more tunefully but not more pleasantly. This time she sang with a low-pitched, breathy sound reminiscent of Marlene Dietrich's cabaret moan, which I had always found distasteful.

The song was "Poor Butterfly." Or, more precisely, she sang the melody for that song but apparently didn't know the lyrics except for the line, "And I must die, poor butterfly," which she kept repeating with little interspersed passages of humming. Her cheek was cold against mine.

We danced clumsily, our bare feet catching in the frayed rug. Elizabeth seemed to be acting out something from her experience. I wanted to know if it was literal or symbolic.

"Elizabeth," I said, "what does the song about the butterfly mean to you?"

She didn't answer but kept humming. I wasn't sure she had heard me. I tried again. "Who sang the song?"

"No one sang it."

"And you don't know the words. Then what does it mean?"

"Meta . . . mor . . . pho . . . sis."

"Metamorphosis? From what to what?"

Elizabeth began humming "Poor Butterfly" again.

"What about the other song? The rock-and-roll song?"

"Before."

"Before what?"

The humming began again. There didn't seem to be any point in asking more questions, but I tried once again. "What was the metamorphosis?"

Elizabeth whispered what sounded like "Eva."

"Eva?" I said.

"No. Ava."

"Who is Ava?"

I could feel Elizabeth growing weaker, and suddenly she collapsed heavily against me. I half carried her to her bed and put my fingertips against her wrist. Her pulse was erratic. It was producing an uneven pattern consisting of a flurry of quick beats and slow thuds separated by abnormally long pauses. Her hands were cold.

"Shall I call an ambulance?" I asked. Elizabeth shook her head no. "A doctor? Is there a doctor who will come?"

"The nurse," she said, and pointed to an address book on her bedside table. I handed it to her, and she found me a number for a Nurse LeTourneau. I dialed the number. An answering machine referred me to another number, which got me to Registered Nurse LeTourneau, who sounded tough and cynical, as I thought all nurses should sound. I described Elizabeth's condition.

"She'll be all right," the nurse said. "There should be some pills in the drawer of the bedside table." I opened the drawer and found a prescription container. I read the label to the nurse. "That's it," she said. "Give her two of those. If she's not better by the morning, call me again." I thanked the nurse. She paused. "What brought it on?" she asked. It was my turn to pause. Then Nurse LeTourneau asked, "Were you dancing?" I admitted that we had been. "I've

done that, too," she said. "It's not to be encouraged
. . . night-night."

The medication stabilized Elizabeth's heartbeat
almost immediately, and she fell into a sound sleep. I
picked up the two robes. Before I put them back in the
closet, I tried each of them on. They were not only old
but were slightly threadbare as if they had been worn
frequently over the years. They were a little small for
me, but I thought they would have fit Eva and David
when the twins were in their late teens—when Bill
Haley's recording of "Rock Around the Clock" was
popular.

But what about "Poor Butterfly"? There was obviously something in Elizabeth's past that was torment-
ing her. I wondered if it had to do with the twins. If so,
it seemed likely that David's role was more important
than Eva's. *Role* seemed like the appropriate term for
David; more than most of us, he was playing a part. If
I knew his role, maybe I could prevent Elizabeth from
being ill and behaving strangely. I wanted only to be
alone with her, reading to her or saying commonplace
things on a quiet Midwestern night as the year neared
its end. We were closer than mother and daughter—
closer than father and daughter—for we were not
together by chance. We had chosen to be with each
other. If there was unpleasantness in the night, it was
not of our doing. We were its victims.

I sat until dawn, sleepily guarding Elizabeth. Under
my care, she slept peacefully and with dignity and
beauty.

21 | *A Revelation in the Attic*

I was still at Elizabeth's side the next morning at eight o'clock when the telephone rang. It was David Dobb, who said he wanted to speak to his mother. His oddly pitched voice sounded even stranger on the telephone than it did in person. It was like a computer-generated tape that was running a little too fast.

"I don't think your mother should talk now," I said. "She had a bad night."

"How bad, Jillian? Very bad, perhaps?" David was trying to sound gleeful at the prospect, but I still didn't believe he meant his mother harm.

"Not too bad, I think. She got overstimulated."

"Too much company, by any chance? I understand my sister and her dim-bulb daughter have invaded . . . not to mention your father. Was naughty Matthew the source of the overstimulation?"

"Did you just call to be unpleasant, or do you want me to take a message for Elizabeth?"

"Actually, while I have you—so to speak—maybe you'll agree to eat lunch with me soon. I have a proposition to put to you."

"If it's the usual proposition, you needn't bother, David. You don't ever have to bother."

"I'm disappointed in your lack of sexual imagination, my dear, but I'm beginning to accept it. What I have to propose to you concerns something that you find more arousing than sex."

"I'm not looking for *any* kind of arousal at the moment. I just want to do my job without distractions."

"This has to do with your job. I guarantee you'll be interested. But it can wait until Thanksgiving, I suppose. That's the message you can give my mother. I'm taking the week off, and I plan to be a house guest in the ancestral barn. That is, if there is still an unoccupied bedroom there by then. And on the chance that you might have an attack of curiosity before then, I won't cancel my luncheon reservation for two tomorrow."

David gave me a time and place. I hesitated. Perhaps I should see him tomorrow on the principle of "know your enemy."

David said, "Weakening?"

"Goodbye," I said, and hung up. But I wondered whether it was true that I was weakening in some essential way. People are like spiders, I thought. They seem individual and self-concerned, but each person is surrounded by a web in which he or she hopes to trap the innocent or careless passerby. David's web was large and dangerous.

Elizabeth seemed to sleep through the phone call, but as soon as I replaced the receiver, she said, "Was that David?"

"Yes. But it wasn't important." I didn't want to distress her with the news about his Thanksgiving visit, which was only about a week away. I said, "What's important is how you feel."

"I feel regenerated. But I'm tired."

"You should rest today. You've had too much excitement lately."

"I suppose you're right. I am less resolute since you have lived with me—less able to control my affairs."

"That's the way it should be, Elizabeth. I will take control. I will control the people surrounding you, but it is more difficult for me to control the impulses within you. I was caught off guard by your behavior last night."

"I dare say. There is still much you don't know about me . . . and about my family."

"I'll find out. Yes. I must learn more."

I got a breakfast tray for Elizabeth, and I warned Eva and Shirley not to bother her for the rest of the day. After breakfast, Elizabeth fell into another profound sleep. I wanted to learn more about the family, but I didn't want to question Eva. I felt the need of solitude. I wanted to lie on my bed with a collection of pictures and documents—a family history—and read and reflect.

I stopped in to see Father, who was in bed under a thick down comforter and who looked as exhausted as Elizabeth. I knew he had not slept much the night before because I hadn't heard the elaborate snores he produces when he's sleeping soundly (a sign of virility, he claims). Instead, I had heard the faint, rhythmic clicking made by his keyboard when he is playing it with the speakers turned off. One of the reasons Father looked old and vulnerable in the bed was that his body was covered. He had the kind of body that does not draw attention to itself but that unobtrusively creates a sense of strength.

"Do you want me to read to you?" I asked.

"No. I'll be asleep in one and a half minutes. What'll you be up to?"

"I was going to see if I could find out some more about the Dobb family without getting involved with its members."

"Is there a library downstairs?"

"No. Not as such."

Father said, "Then try the attic." Almost immediately he began to snore.

The attic was lighted by two small, low-strength light bulbs. There were no windows, and the only other light came from a few small chinks in the neglected roof and walls. As I had expected, the attic was filled with hundreds of objects, but I was surprised to find that most of the objects seemed to have been thrown together randomly, forming a series of large, vague mounds that were interspersed with footpaths. I stood for a few minutes letting my eyes adjust to the feeble light. My breath formed tiny clouds of vapor in the chill air, and the only sounds I could hear were from outside the house—an occasional barking dog, a bleating car horn, or a screeching child.

Given the time and interest, I could have played archeologist-historian and reconstructed a century in the history of the Dobb family by sifting through these midden heaps. Or at least I could have compiled an impersonal history, for as I began to distinguish objects within the jumble of material, it was obvious that they represented people's purchases and not their thoughts. I could see nothing that might be correspondence or a journal.

Father says that the only thing that has kept the United States from having a mass nervous breakdown is that Americans not only acquire things, but they also throw them away. We want things, but we still realize that the things will not bring us salvation. The aphorism Father has worked out is: "Craziness begins when disposal stops." He talks about the Collyer brothers, whose sanity was submerged by objects. He talks about the Orson Welles character in the movie *Citizen Kane,* who sinks under the weight of his acquisitions.

The attic made me think of the ending of *Citizen Kane,* in which vast quantities of the dead publisher's possessions are being destroyed. I could even see, protruding from one of the Dobb mounds, a sled. I moved closer to it to see if there was any symbol painted on it, but found only the words "Flexible Flyer." Yet any of the objects that were around

me—objects that seemed innocuous and worthless—
might once have had unimaginable meaning for someone in the Dobb family. I was in a museum full of
objects valuable not in themselves but for the emotions that had once been invested in them.

I pulled a dress from the top of one of the mounds.
It had probably been worn by someone in the 1920s. It
was frivolous: short, tubular, fringed. Someone might
have been seduced or abandoned while wearing it.

Clothing once worn by other people seemed to me
to have power. I was disturbed whenever I passed a
thrift shop or a church bazaar and saw people casually
and thoughtlessly sorting through and trying on used
clothing. Apparently most people fail to sense what I
detect in old garments: a residue of the original
owner's personality and experience. We are careless
about such things. I am sure there are simpler, more
sensitive societies in which discarded clothing is
treated reverentially: burned ritually, buried with a
deceased owner.

I thought of the tunic Mrs. Ellis had given me. It
was more than a memento. It was part of her being
and knowledge. It was a source of power for me.

I looked more carefully at the dress that was in my
hand. It was a party dress. There would have been
little or nothing worn between it and its owner's
(Elizabeth's?) body. It would have been stained by
illicit whiskey or gin. It was an object to stimulate the
senses. I could understand the persistent appeal of
transvestism or the impulse of certain men to insist
that the prostitute dress up in a girl scout uniform.

I dropped the dress where I had found it, and as I
did so, I noticed something peculiar about the heaps.
One would have expected the material to be arranged
more or less chronologically, with the older objects on
the bottom. But that was not the case. Scattered along
the tops of all the heaps were items of women's
clothing that seemed to be from all eras: a floor-

length, long-sleeved dress; a miniskirt; a straw cloche; a corset; a sling pump.

The objects in the attic, I thought, must once have been neatly arranged. But someone had rummaged through them, looking for something—perhaps the women's garments visible now.

Someone in the Dobb family had understood the power or felt the stimulation of another's clothing. I recalled the poem I had read to Elizabeth—the one that had been marked in her book of ballads, and I remembered her request for the passage from *Jane Eyre*—both connected with cross-dressing. Did someone in the Dobb house enjoy trying on old dresses? I made my way through the disorder, letting my eye be taken by objects at random: a floor-model radio, its wood cabinet split; a metal-framed lawn chair; *Life* magazines; a pleated lampshade; a chipped terra-cotta pot; broken 78-rpm phonograph records.

Half hidden by one of the mounds of material was a graceful writing desk that, judging from its unmarked finish, seemed hardly to have been used. It had probably been consigned to the attic as soon as it had been purchased, because its delicate, gently curved legs and undecorated surface were so at odds with the solid assertiveness of the house and the rest of its contents. I cleared a space around the desk and ran my fingers over the glassily smooth wood. I traced my name in its dust. The desk was from a time when someone who had studied Latin would compose formal messages on handmade paper in carefully formed script. The designer had echoed the object's purpose; from where I had first seen it, the desk had resembled a carefully written character from an unfamiliar alphabet.

I lifted the brass handle at the front of the desk and pulled out a wide, shallow drawer. At the left of the drawer was a neat stack of note paper which turned out, unfortunately, to be blank. On the right was a box which had once been filled with chocolates but now contained dozens of loose snapshots. Taking the box to an area beneath one of the ceiling lights, I sat down on an old hassock and began to look quickly through the photographs. They depicted only a few periods of Elizabeth's life—apparently the years immediately before and after her marriage to Andrew Dobb. The basic truth of Elizabeth's relationship to her husband was obvious in the pictures. The dominant emotions were aversion and fear. Elizabeth always stood apart from or leaned away from her husband. The two were like magnets with their positive poles facing. They repelled each other with strong, invisible forces.

I thought it odd that even though many of the pictures had been taken late in Elizabeth's marriage, the twins did not appear in any of them. Surely the twins had been photographed—young children inspire almost anyone to pick up a camera. I wondered if someone had removed such pictures from the collection. What I found much odder, though, was a group portrait of Elizabeth and six other women. They were wearing bathing suits. The picture was no larger or more formal than the others, and most people would have found it unremarkable. But it unsettled me. It had the occult overtones that even the most innocent photographs can have; the mysterious implications found in any moment of a former life, even one's own. The picture must have been taken at a reunion: seven middle-aged, half-naked women, some with arms linked, some with a hand on another's shoulder. They showed the slight embarrassment and excitement of people who were not used to wearing bathing suits and who were not comfortable touching one another. They stood at the edge of an untended field, and judging from the harsh light and long, deep shadows, it was late afternoon of a summer day. Were they at the lakeside? Where was the beach? The photo could have been a frame from a surrealistic movie of the 1930s.

But what disturbed me most about the portrait was not its incongruous qualities but the women it depicted. One of the subjects was Elizabeth Dobb. The six other women resembled the companions I had lived with before I came to Serena—the women I had heard in the séance at Mrs. Tickle's. It was impossible, of course, that they could have been those women. My employer/companions had lived in widely scattered areas of the Midwest; their ages were not as closely matched as the ages of the women in the photo; and I knew that many of my companions had never left their hometowns.

But the photograph seemed to symbolize something I had long believed—that there were connections among my companions; that I was predestined to offer them my services.

The photograph was a validation of my acts of recent years. It was a sign, an omen, but I wasn't sure whether or not it was propitious. I opened the top buttons of my blouse and tucked the photo into my bra over my left breast.

I returned the other pictures to the desk in which I had found them, and as I did so I noticed at the back of the drawer a book bound in imitation leather and inscribed, "Serena Regional High School, Class of 1959." That was probably the year of the twins' graduation. I lifted the book, pulling it free of two bent, unburned candles that were stuck to its back cover. As I opened it, an unpleasant, fetid odor was released. The pages were rippled and stuck together along the edges, and I pried them apart at random, revealing head-and-shoulder photographs of people who looked remarkably alike, the young men with crew cuts and the young women (photographed three-quarter view) with pony tails.

I turned to the "D" pages, and, as I expected, there were pictures of the twins. But there was something unexpected: the captions read "Eva" and "Ava Dobb."

In 1959, David Dobb had been called Ava Dobb and was on the girls' swimming team.

I put the yearbook back in the drawer and stood leaning against the desk while the shock of my discovery did various things to my nervous system. I realized that I was laughing. Would someone in the family awaken in terror, remembering the novels and movies in which the laughter of the ghost or the mad wife drifted through the dark corridors of the old house? If so, that person would most likely drift quickly back to sleep in the knowledge that things are often not what they seem to be, that we live among illusions.

22 | *How David Grew*

For the first time, David was of intense interest to me, and I decided to accept his luncheon invitation. I called him at his office and arranged to meet him there the following day. Next I called John Ellis and asked him if he would drive me into Chicago so that I could meet David. John agreed. Then I went to Elizabeth's room.

As I waited for Elizabeth to wake up, I thought about David Dobb. At the time he graduated from high school—in his late teens—he had apparently been a woman, Eva Dobb's identical twin. Was he simply pretending to be a man now? No. I had danced with him; I knew that he had no breasts and that he had at least a rudimentary beard. He must have had some sort of surgery after leaving high school. I had heard of such things, but they usually involved men who wanted to become women. And they were usually in Hollywood or Stockholm or New York City, not in small-town Iowa.

I didn't speculate about why David—or Ava—might have wanted to become a man. I had encountered enough distinctive sexual impulses—in myself and in others—to conclude that sexual orientation just happens. And being an identical twin introduces piquant elements into the sexual equation. I wondered about Eva's tendencies. What I couldn't help wondering about, however, was David's body. I wanted to know whether he had a penis and, if so, whether it was serviceable.

Elizabeth awakened with a smile. I have found that the most profoundly appreciated act a companion can perform is to be waiting at the bedside when her employer awakens. Some people believe that the soul leaves the body and wanders during sleep, and that a person who is awakened suddenly can lose his or her soul. It is reassuring, especially if you are an old person, to be welcomed back to the world of consciousness by someone who wants your life to have meaning and symmetry—by a soulmate.

I brought Elizabeth her juice and coffee, and I waited until she had bathed before I talked to her about David. She asked me to wash her back, a ritual we were both becoming fond of, but one that I let her initiate. Bathing has always been important to me, both as a symbolic act and as an intensely pleasing activity. My first sexual experiences—masturbatory—were in a tubful of warm water, and I have never enjoyed sex with a person whose body was not clean. A deformed but clean body has more appeal to me than one that is perfectly formed but soiled.

The physical and sexual thoughts I had as I helped Elizabeth bathe were entwined with thoughts of David/Ava. I still felt unsettled and somewhat aroused by what I had discovered.

As Elizabeth was dressing, there was a knock on the door that led to Father's room, and he said, "Anyone home?"

"Hand me my robe," Elizabeth said.

"You're forgetting," I said to her. "It's not necessary." I called to Father, "Come in."

When he was in the room, I said, "Elizabeth's not decent."

"These are the times I feel handicapped," Father said.

Elizabeth dressed quickly. Father, as I suspected,

was aware that there had been a problem the night before. "Everyone's health okay?" he asked.

"I think so," I said, and looked questioningly at Elizabeth. She held out her arm to me, and I put my fingertips on her wrist. Her pulse was strong, but there was a slight irregularity in the rhythm. I took Father's hand and put it on Elizabeth's wrist.

"It's like a waltz the way the Vienna Philharmonic plays it. Subtle hesitations." As Father released Elizabeth's wrist, his hand brushed against her hip. "Seem decent enough to me," he muttered. Then, dramatically, he said, "Elizabeth, what you need is some good, old-fashioned, hands-on faith healing. Maybe combined with some immersion. You'll be as good as new."

"I wouldn't enjoy feeling new at my age, Matthew."

"Would a healthy forty be acceptable?"

"A healthy sixty would be perfect."

"I can arrange it," Father said. "Just say when. Not now, though. Mary's going to give me some navigation lessons around the house. It's a complicated layout." He left the room.

Elizabeth looked uncomprehending. "Mary?"

"The housekeeper," I said.

Elizabeth produced a disapproving "Hmmph" and sat down. I took a chair opposite her and went to the point.

"Let me know if this subject upsets you, and I'll stop."

"What subject?" Elizabeth clasped her hands tightly together in her lap.

"I saw the twins' high school yearbook."

Elizabeth smiled and looked relieved. "And you're thinking David has changed somewhat," she said. "That's not one of my favorite subjects, but it doesn't upset me. It's just a bad joke I've heard too often." She paused to look for my reaction, then continued. "Although the causes are, I suppose, endlessly complicated, the effects are simple enough. Eva's identical twin, Ava (their father named them), decided after leaving high school that she wanted to enter college as a man. Her father said he'd always regretted not having had a son (he blamed me for that, of course), and that he wanted someone to look after his money. He thought, naturally, that women were not to be trusted with money, even though I had always been financially responsible and was never extravagant. But my idiotic husband financed an expensive and elaborate operation." Elizabeth paused before asking, "Is this credible to you, Jillian?"

"I suppose so. It's apparently undeniable."

"Oh yes. I never tried to deny it to myself or anyone who took the trouble to ask. But I must refer you to David for the details. I accept him as my offspring, but not as a son. To me, he is merely an extremely silly close relative. For a time, I felt resentful of his silliness, but he has paid the price for it, and now he seems pathetic."

"Paid the price?"

"Yes. Literally. At the center of his life now is this enormous irony. His father left a bequest to 'my only son.' I contested the will on the grounds that David was only nominally a son, that biologically he was a woman and therefore did not meet the terms of the will. I won, although probably for the wrong reasons. The court realized that my husband's intention was to leave some money to David. But the judge was morally offended by David's act and wanted to punish him for it. The judge was a woman, and she may have believed that David had betrayed womankind."

"What about Eva?" I asked. "Did she inherit anything?"

"No. That's another reason I contested the will; it didn't mention a daughter or daughters. I inherited everything—on the grounds that next to a son, a known evil such as a wife was a safer guardian of wealth than a still-developing daughter. But I gave Eva the amount designated for the 'son.'"

"Then David is not legally a man?"

"No. Psychologically he may be some sort of man, but legally—and physically, I suspect—he is not."

I wondered whether David had been unreasonably punished for his attempt at a sex change, especially considering that his father had encouraged it. I said, "I can see why David might not be very fond of you."

"He probably despises me, but he doesn't show it. He visits me often—too often—and he's never nasty. He *does* ask for money, but he smiles when he asks. Behind the smile, though, I occasionally see a threat in his eyes. When we're alone in the house, I feel I should be holding a handgun at all times. But usually I don't give him a thought."

"Are you sure, Elizabeth? What about 'Poor Butterfly' and the metamorphosis the other night? Wasn't that about Ava/David?"

"Yes. But that doesn't happen often. It's a course correction that I make."

"The robes were Ava/David's?"

"Yes. Before and after the operation—the metamorphosis, a reverse metamorphosis in which the beautiful butterfly becomes an ugly, wormlike creature. Poor butterfly."

"But David's not ugly."

"Morally he is, but not physically, no."

"What did the surgery involve?"

Elizabeth raised her palms, an elaborate gesture for her. "I don't know the disgusting details. A double mastectomy and a complete hysterectomy plus some hormones, I believe."

"He must have suffered."

"We all suffer. She—or he—was young, strong, and manic."

I had to ask, "Does David have a penis?"

"Good heavens, Jillian. Why concern yourself with

that? If you feel you must know, ask David. He certainly likes us to think he has such a thing. I believe he takes women—undiscriminating women—to bed. But I have no idea what he subjects them to . . . perhaps just an unpleasant surprise. And now, as an old woman says in an Oscar Wilde play, that's all there is to say on *that* subject." Elizabeth was smiling. I didn't know whether she was thinking about *The Importance of Being Earnest* or about being asked whether her son had a penis.

23 | *Let the*
Good Times Roll

The drive to Chicago with John Ellis was restorative. I had not slept well in several days, and as we drove through the clear-horizoned countryside, I closed my eyes against the brightness of the sun, which was reflecting off a dusting of snow. My consciousness ebbed and flowed as John recited a comforting monologue. I unbuttoned my coat, and he reached over occasionally and rested his right hand on my thigh, allowing his warmth to penetrate the thin material of my dress.

"You're leaving Mrs. Dobb alone for the day?" John asked.

"Hardly. She has an excess of companionship these days. Her daughter and granddaughter and my father have all moved in."

"What's the attraction, the old lady or you?"

"The combination, maybe. People might sense the bond between me and Elizabeth—the unusual bond —and might want to share it."

"What's so unusual about it?"

"It's a spiritual bond."

"Is that what you form with all your old ladies?"

"More or less. Spiritual affection."

"I don't know how you can stand to see them die."

"It's not like affection between young people. It's a triangle, with death as the rival."

"And the rival always wins. Don't you get tired of losing?"

"Everybody loses eventually. It's a matter of losing gracefully."

"But *you* don't lose. And *death* doesn't lose. The *old ladies* lose."

"My time will come."

John made a rude noise with his lips. "Jillian, why don't you give this stuff up? You've got something unusual, but why don't you use it in the real world?"

"You're sweet, John, but your idea of the real world is all mixed up with the world of TV commercials, where there aren't any shadows. But this country, especially the heartland, was developed in the shadows."

"You ought to go to see a few baseball games. We get rid of the shadows. We put up lights. And the whole point of the game is that everybody doesn't always lose. The point is that on any given day the worst team might win; the worst pitcher may throw a shutout; the worst batter may go four for four."

In his concern with his metaphor, John had forgotten about touching my body. But he was still reaching out to me in a sense. He was like a boy in his secret clubhouse saying things to another boy—things he wouldn't say to his parents.

"It's easy for the umpire to talk about winning and losing," I said. "But he's not a player. He never really knows what it means to win or lose."

"Then make me a winner. Come and live with me. I've got a nice house. I'm fun-loving. We could have good times." John let his dream carry him away. He started to sing in a Ray Charles-ish voice: "Just let the good times roll, babe."

His dream wasn't without appeal to me. I might enjoy responding to the demands of his athlete's body and his simple good humor. But I was sure the appeal would fade quickly. Rather than explain that to John, I simply said, "Mrs. Dobb needs me. She's ill."

"No problem there. Let Matthew take care of her. He's already living with her. He could dust off the old faith-healing techniques and make her healthy. And then he could be companionable in your place. *You* could be *my* companion."

"You'd feel safe with me?"

"Sure. I'd make you so happy that you'd want to make sure I lived forever. And besides, I can take care of myself."

His self-deception was disturbing, but I was too sleepy and comfortable to argue with him. "I'll think about it, John," I said.

I closed my eyes again and raised my skirt. John's hand went to my thigh. My consciousness sank to the level just above sleep. John's hand moved lightly over me. Through my eyelids, I sensed the change in the intensity of light caused by a few cottony clouds that drifted across the sun.

I tried to imagine what it would be like to be married to John Ellis. My imaginings in that area usually ended quickly and negatively, as they had during my recent talk with Father. John was too much like my ex-husband. They were both obsessed with their occupations. Actually, the fact that they made a living of sorts was a by-product of their obsessions. If I were to marry again, which was improbable at best, I would marry someone who not only was free of obsessions but was without a passionate interest in anything—someone whose personality was a featureless expanse of gray, damp clay that I could carve and impress. Otherwise, the person would have to be physically dependent on me, as Father was.

People with passionate interests are attractive. Lovers always think they can commandeer another's passions, that they can take someone's passion for baseball or music or gambling or whatever and transfer it to themselves. We would all like to be the object of the kind of devotion and attention that an alcoholic lavishes on alcohol. But I have known more drunks than lovers.

John Ellis, I thought, should marry someone like Eva Dobb, with whom he had virtually nothing in common. He could watch his baseball games while she invented buildings, and they wouldn't interfere with each other's happiness.

As we drove that day, John's hand was on my body, but his mind was probably on the baseball rule book. I would have been happier if he had been thinking about me and caressing the book.

As we neared Chicago, John asked me for more specific instructions about where we were headed. Finally, he asked for the information I hadn't volunteered. "What are you going to do in the city?"

"I'm meeting a man for lunch."

John's grip became tighter on the wheel. He drove in silence for a mile or two and then said, "Anyone I know?"

"Yes. David Dobb."

His grip relaxed. "Business?"

"No. Pleasure of sorts."

"Of sorts is about all you'd get from David."

"You don't see him as a threat?"

"I wouldn't let him near my money."

"But he can sniff around your woman?"

"Are you my woman, Jillian?"

"I'm my own woman, John. I was being theoretical."

"I like you when you're theoretical."

I wondered if John knew more about David than I knew. "How can you be sure David's not a sexual threat? You're just guessing."

"I can be pretty sure. The night we were all at Walter's, David and I were in the john together. He has to squat to pee."

24 | *Ladies Who Lunch*

John dropped me at David's office building and headed off to his own luncheon appointment, which was with a baseball statistician who, because he refused to use a computer, was in unadmitted retirement. John and I were to meet later in the afternoon and drive back to Serena together.

The city's hyperactive crowds frightened me. The financial-district yuppies swarmed around me; they seemed to be involved in the kind of intense, mindless activity that takes place in a nursery-school playground during recess.

I think it's dangerous in many ways for large numbers of people to gather together in public. The individual's personality seems not, as one might expect, to become submerged, but is intensified as if it wants to assert its superiority to the personalities that surround it. People are least dangerous when they spend most of their time in couples or small groups, which allows them to behave subtly. David Dobb fit my theory. His desk was in a glass-fronted office that faced a large room crowded with desks, telephones, computer terminals, and young people who were almost identically dressed and who wore almost identical expressions of ambition and aggressiveness. Although there were almost as many women as men in the office, the uniformity extended to gender, and the sexual ambiguity in the staff must have pleased David.

The dominant emotions in the office seemed to be anger and near hysteria.

David carried the ambience of the office into the restaurant he had chosen. We had arrived, at my request, unfashionably early, so that there might be some time for us to talk intimately before the crowd noise became too distracting. But David was not in a placid mood. I hoped the vodka he ordered (poured from a bottle encased in a block of ice) would tranquilize him a bit. Because I wasn't at my most tranquil either, I accepted some of the vodka.

It is not my manner to stare at a companion. I prefer to lower my eyes frequently and to gaze intensely only occasionally and briefly when trying to interpret a person's mood or the meaning of a specific remark. But I was seeing David in a new light, of course, and it was difficult for me to keep from conducting a detailed physical examination of him. I decided that despite my new knowledge about David, I still saw him as a man. For some reason, I thought that if I could put my hands on him I would be able to confirm for myself his essential manliness. When he greeted me at the office, he had ignored my offer of a handshake and had kissed my cheek.

As David studied the menu, I studied his hands. His fingers certainly seemed stronger and larger-boned than his sister Eva's. Could his hands have been altered? Or could exercise have changed them in a fundamental way? I wanted David to say something charming so that I could reach out and take his hand without seeming uncharacteristically drawn to him. His choice of food didn't endear him to me. "I'm going to have the veal chop with raisin and coriander sauce," he said. "I recommend it."

"I have a small-town palate," I said. "I'll just have a green salad and broiled lake trout. I've never understood why people make such a fuss over food. They

156

seem to expect so much more than sustenance from it."

David gave me his affectionately superior look—his right eyebrow and the right corner of his mouth raised. "I suspect you don't see the need to indulge any of your appetites, Jillian. You're an ascetic, like many people with a mission."

"And what's my mission?"

"Why don't we order before we get into that?"

The waiter insisted that a cranberry and caper cream sauce should be served with my fish, and I said I didn't care what kind of sauce he brought as long as it was in a separate sauce boat that I could ignore. Before deciding on the wine, David had a silly little discussion with a sommelier who hardly seemed to be of drinking age. I turned my wine glass over and ordered more vodka.

"You were going to describe my mission," I said to David.

He reached over and took my hand. I looked away and concentrated on the sensation of touch, as though I were Father. I felt as if I were being touched by a man—a fastidious but not effeminate man. I also felt slightly aroused by the oddness of the situation.

"I'm going to speak to you in terms you've tried to avoid, my dear. No euphemisms today." David finished his vodka. "You're a psychopath, a serial murderer who kills old ladies and justifies it to herself by saying her victims are better off dead."

I tried to withdraw my hand, but David clung to it. His words seemed meaningless to me—meaningless but unpleasant. I saw no need to reply.

"And you're probably right in most cases. You're certainly right in my mother's case."

"We're in a public place," I said.

"Nobody listens to anyone else in these places—not even to the person they're with. But I hope you'll pay attention to me, Jillian. I want you to go ahead and do away with your companion Elizabeth. I'll reward you, and I'll send you on your way. But I want it to be soon, my dear."

Except for the almost bruising firmness of his grip, David seemed to be receding from me. I wasn't sure I understood him. He sipped his vodka and then continued. "You're going to do it anyway. I'm just asking you to hurry."

"I don't know what you're talking about," I said.

"I suppose you don't. I suppose psychologists would call it some kind of denial. Let me try this. What if the police in the town you just left were told where you are? I know they want to talk to you. I'm sure many police in many towns want to talk to you."

Our salads arrived, and David stopped babbling for a moment. I had known that David wanted to use me, but until his announcement I hadn't known how. I had expected something more imaginative of him, but it was clear now that his exoticism was just a facade covering simple greed, just as the elaborate facades on the houses John and Eva were so impassioned about concealed simple wooden boxes.

I knew that David didn't really believe the things he had just said about me. He was consciously distorting the facts to benefit himself. To call me a murderer was like saying that a priest giving the last rites was a murderer. David was purposely misstating my role; he was using the language that insensitive bureaucrats would use.

All of us have events in our backgrounds that would lead to difficulties if they were known to unsympathetic people. And certainly David was vulnerable. When the waiter had served the salad, I said to David, "I saw your picture in your high school yearbook."

David closed his left eye and rubbed it. "Okay . . . I concede," he said, and smiled. "I'll have to plan around you. But in a few hours or a few days, you'll probably remember the things I've just said. They'll seem clearer than they do now. Think about them seriously, and if you decide you want to get some details, let me know." He finished his vodka, poured himself some wine, and asked, with a grin, "Now, about that yearbook picture. Would you say I've changed much?"

"It's hard to say. I didn't know you then. And I don't know you very well now."

"Even though you're not being very cooperative with me, Jillian, I'd be glad to let you know me better. I'll let you know me as well as you'd like."

"Your mother thinks you say that to all the girls."

"Not at all. I like to watch women—almost any woman—take their clothes off. But that's just a little idiosyncrasy. It has nothing to do with friendship. I like to *look* on a man-to-woman basis, but to *talk* woman-to-woman."

"Then this is a ladies' lunch."

"Yes, but that's our secret."

I didn't have to ask David about his sex change. He chattered on about it freely, even after the adjoining tables were occupied.

"I'm just being a modern woman," he said. "We're expected to compete with men; why not become a man? My dear sister tried it the other way. She tried to have a career and a husband, and now she has neither. We both knew that our father wanted a son, and we both tried to accommodate him, but Eva took half-measures."

I knew David wasn't telling the whole story. For example, there was no mention of the blocked inheritance. Also, he didn't volunteer any details about the current components of his anatomy, but he said he'd be glad to arrange a show-and-tell session during his Thanksgiving visit.

I thought I had received David's explanation uncritically, but he eventually said, "You don't approve, do you, Jillian?"

"It's not that I disapprove, it's just that I still don't understand why you did it."

"Became a man, you mean? I wouldn't have expected you to have any trouble with that. I don't get the impression that you're devoted to old-fashioned feminine qualities like submission and compassion. Come off it, Jillian. Admit that you're not the type, any more than I was, to be interested in getting fucked by the mailman or in cleaning off smudges around light switches."

I said, "Women are allowed to do other things these days—things like chairing boards of directors."

"Yes. I've been to those board meetings. The men sit there waiting for the chairperson to excuse herself because her period has started. Men still have the real power, Jillian. I wanted some of it."

David's concept of power was not as broad as mine. I thought I might have a power that was beyond his. "I suppose you're right," I said.

"The man always *is* right, my dear. But we're talking woman-to-woman, aren't we?"

I sat back and listened as David began to talk about other things. He was witty and attentive, and soon I began to enjoy his company, learning his views on such subjects as politics (the presidency will soon be televised for two hours each afternoon, "brought to us by grants from major corporations"), pets (they're for people who haven't learned any other way to gain a sense of superiority), and music (it will become increasingly important as we become a nonverbal, number-manipulating society).

After lunch, we walked back to David's office building, where John was to pick me up. As we walked, I tried to remember the remarks David had made about me at lunch, but I could remember nothing specific. As David predicted, I was to recall the remarks later, but at that time I could only remember them as being distasteful to me.

25 | *Having My Way*

During the drive back to Serena, John was not disturbed by my silence, because I unbuckled my seat belt and moved close to him and allowed him to place his hand wherever he could reach.

"This is dangerous for you," he said. "A one-handed driver and no seat belt."

"There are always dangers, John."

"Some of us love danger."

"Are you in that category?"

"I love *you.*"

"Well, I'm certainly dangerous. David Dobb just told me that."

"I hate to admit it, but he's right. You're weird and dangerous."

Was John right? Was I those things? Maybe no one thinks of herself or himself as weird and dangerous. But some people *are* those things. I said, "I prefer to think of myself as interesting and distinctive . . . as my own person."

"But not as dangerous?"

"Not to you, John."

I would have had a different answer for David Dobb.

John and I settled into silence. But when we got back to Serena, John once again demonstrated his passionate boyishness. He had discovered the backroad clump of woods that served as Serena's lovers' lane. We stopped there at dusk on our way back from

162

Chicago, and John surprised me by chastely putting his hand on my shoulder and asking me to marry him. Unlike his earlier proposition that we live together, this was a formal proposal.

It was time I ended these little discussions with John, time I dissolved his hopes. "No, John," I said. "I'll never marry you. It's understandable that you think you love me. I've involved you in serious matters. I've turned you away from the sunny surface and allowed you to see some of the shadows. You feel profound. You think I'm a sorcerer. But you don't want to be the sorcerer's apprentice; you want me to become the umpire's groupie. Can you really imagine me sitting in back of first base and caring whether you were right about a close call?"

John seemed to be blushing beneath the remains of his tan. He took his hand from my shoulder. "You don't take me seriously."

"Seriousness isn't the issue. The issue is that you wouldn't risk being seen as evil."

"Unlike you."

"Yes. You're unlike me, John."

"What's so great about being evil?"

"Nothing. I'm not talking about *being* evil. I'm talking about the worthwhile actions that unreflective people see as evil. Many people don't fulfill their lives because they don't want to get near the dividing line."

"Do you ever think you're crazy? That you talk funny? That you're pompous?"

"No. But it's all right if you think that about me."

John was so upset that he didn't even try to make love to me. I insisted on walking home alone, and I left him sitting in the car. I wanted to forget about the city and about David and John. I walked clumsily through the growing darkness, invigorated by the cold and the silence. I felt as if I were a member of a religious order. I was undergoing a little ritual of rededication.

As I moved along the side of the road to town, John's car, unlighted, came up suddenly behind me. The car was moving fast, and it passed within a foot of me. But to an umpire, missing your target by a foot isn't even coming close. I wondered if the gesture was John's way of saying goodbye.

After about ten minutes, I began to feel less virtuous and spiritual about my decision to walk to town. I've never felt at home in nature, and I believe that whatever the actual differences are between men and women, one of them is that men are uniquely drawn to contact with the elements. In recent weeks, I had seen hunters prowling the fields and woods near Serena, and I thought their pleasure came not so much from stalking and shooting as from being more intimate than usual with the earth and air.

Even now, I suspected, there was probably a man nearby who was pleased (as I was not) that the wind was rising and shifting (probably to the north) and that clouds were beginning to obscure the enormous gray smear of the Milky Way and the rising moon. I associated the outdoors with burial, and as I walked I became not so much frightened as depressed. I wasn't longing for comfort and warmth but for a space with limits—a shelter. I wondered if such a desire on such a night might not have inspired Eva's decision to become an architect.

Then headlights appeared ahead of me. Was John returning? I thought of moving off the road and hiding, but there was no decent cover nearby. I would have had to lie on the ground behind a bush or in a furrow. I kept walking.

The approaching car pulled to a stop a few yards ahead of me, and its headlights went off. Lights went on inside the car, and I saw the word "Police" on a door. On top of the car was a heavy bracket on which were mounted sirens, flashers, and spotlights. One of the spotlights went on, and its beam swept along the road until it rested on me. I turned my back on it.

The light went out, and a man's voice called, "You need some help, lady?"

I didn't know the answer to that question.

"Do you want a lift?" the voice asked.

"Yes," I said. "I think I do."

I walked toward the car, trying to make out the features of the officer in the dim interior light of the car. He was wearing one of those ludicrous Smokey the Bear hats with the flat brim and the high, pinched crown. I couldn't tell what his face looked like. He pushed open the door opposite the driver's seat, and as I slid onto the seat next to him, he said, "I'm Jay Barnett. I'm in charge of law enforcement in Serena."

Officer Barnett took off his hat. His features were gauntly irregular. He seemed exceptionally short-waisted and long-legged. I thought he had probably killed people. I found him attractive.

"I'm Jillian Cole."

"I know."

I raised my eyebrows in surprise.

He said, "It's my job to know who's in Serena and why they're here." He paused for a moment and stared at me unblinkingly. "I'm not sure why you're here," he continued.

"On this road, do you mean? Or in Serena?"

"Both."

"I'm on the road because of a clumsy man, and I'm in Serena by chance."

"Lots of men are clumsy."

"But you're not."

"I'm not clumsy, no. I'm not nice, either."

John Ellis was clumsy and nice, I thought. Officer Barnett would arrest John but not me. "You must be somewhat nice—nice enough to obey the laws."

"I don't obey all of them, and I don't enforce all of them."

"How do you decide which laws to obey and enforce?"

"I play hunches."

"You gamble with people's lives?"

"What do you do with people's lives, Ms. Cole?"

He knows what I do, I thought. *And he doesn't care. He won't disturb my life. He'll take me to the Dobb house, and as I leave him, he'll put his hat on and touch its brim with two fingers.*

"Do you have any hunches about me?" I asked.

"I have knowledge of you."

We had an affinity. He was my reverse image. He was a noncompanion. I was sure he lived alone. He allowed things to run their natural course. I wanted to be in a room with him, where I could gauge him in a human space. There is something distorting about being inside an automobile: the constriction, the unnatural posture it forces on passengers. Father says that when he is in a car, his bowels loosen up because he has assumed the "john posture."

I had begun to feel another, more interesting kind of loosening within me as I looked at the police officer. His impassivity was overwhelming. Did he ever smile? I was certain he would never moan, or even gasp, with pleasure. He knew, as I did, that the pleasure is greater when it is contained.

"Do you live nearby?" I asked.

He didn't answer, but started the car. As we drove, he glanced at me occasionally. His eyes were pale, the skin around them creased into a slight squint. *He looks for secrets,* I thought. He probably knew David Dobb's secret.

We pulled up in front of an unpleasantly plain house, a small-windowed box with the front wall higher than the back wall.

"It looks black in this light."

"It looks black in any light."

I had never seen a black house before.

The moment of decision had arrived. And it was *my* decision. Officer Barnett was looking at me with dispassionate passion. He was a public servant who was used to gauging the desires of the people he served. He was molesting me with his resistance. John Ellis would not understand my decision. Elizabeth would. I got out of the car and walked to the door of the house.

The interior looked like the interior of the hideout cabins used by rustlers in old B cowboy movies on television. The walls were not just unadorned but unpainted. It was a frontier shelter.

Jay Barnett stood in the center of his shelter, prepared to let me have my way with him. My way was to lead him to his bed and lower his trousers and shorts to midthigh, noting with pleasure that his skin was bone-pale and that it had the faint aroma of newly turned earth. He lay motionless and watched me slowly remove my shoes, hose, and panties. *He's like a trap,* I thought, *all patience and contained energy.* I knelt above him, lifting and positioning his penis, which lay stiff against his belly. I settled upon him, my skirt draping over our bareness. We stared into each other's eyes with rare satisfaction as, unseen beneath my skirt, we joined as secretly and intimately as roots and earth.

I kept my orgasms secret from Jay Barnett, who was not unlike me.

26 | *Through Humblest Hands*

I went immediately to Elizabeth's room when I got home. She didn't ask me about my trip to Chicago, and she didn't seem to resent my having been away all day. She sat in a rocking chair in a corner of her room. I sat opposite her, and we looked fondly at each other. She seemed tired and ill.

If her pseudo-son David could have seen her at that moment, he would have been delighted. And John Ellis would have been distressed. I began to realize that either John's or David's wishes for Elizabeth would have to be acted on. The status quo could not continue.

"Matthew tried to explain the chord structure of the blues to me," Elizabeth said. "He was thorough and patient, but I didn't have the strength to follow his explanation." Elizabeth had seemed to be speaking not to me but to an invisible third person. Now she looked at me directly and raised her voice. "Perhaps it's time to put an end to things."

"That's what David thinks."

"Yes. Sooner or later, he'll have his way."

"Then make it later and on your terms rather than his. And besides, the Thanksgiving holiday promises to be particularly absorbing this year. You wouldn't want to miss that."

"There will be convolutions. Yes. But they won't matter if I'm here in my chimney corner. And the doctors have forgotten how to revive me—if they ever knew. It would take something miraculous to get me out of here."

"Then we'll arrange something miraculous. Tonight at midnight. Sleep till then."

Elizabeth smiled as though she thought I was making a joke. She was mistaken. I went to consult with Father and found him lying on his bed and singing, which was usually an indication that he was bored. It was his way of talking to himself.

"I have a commission for you," I said. "And some information to give you."

"I'm ready for both."

"The information is about David," I said, and I told him about the Ava/David transformation.

"Now, that's what I call information," Father said. As I expected, he didn't seem surprised. He looked elated, as if I were confirming something he already half knew. And he was also a little disturbed. "That's something I wish I could see. He fools most people, I gather."

"He fooled me. Even while I was dancing with him."

"He deserves some credit, then."

"He also deserves some debits. He wants to be rid of Elizabeth. That's where the commission comes in. I want you to help her, to make her strong and healthy."

"Do you believe I can do that?"

"I think Elizabeth believes it."

"Okay," Father said. "As long as one of us believes, it's worth a try."

At fifteen minutes before midnight, Father and I entered Elizabeth's room. She lay face down across the top of her bed, sleeping in an undignified but comfortable position. She looked as though she were climbing the rock face of a cliff.

"She's still asleep," I said. "Shall I wake her up?"

"She doesn't have to be awake, and it'll be less

embarrassing—for all of us—this way. You don't have to stay if you don't want to."

"I'll stay in case she wakes up."

"It would probably be better that way. I might get carried away. I might start talking in tongues, which is nasty stuff, although I try to make it sound like scat singing."

I wondered how serious Father was about this attempt to heal Elizabeth's heart condition. I doubt whether he would have tried it if he didn't think he could do it, but he insisted on making jokes about the laying on of hands.

"You're sure she doesn't have to be conscious?" I asked.

"No, no. I know what you're thinking: this rules out auto-suggestion and hypnosis as an explanation. A psychic investigator told me about that once. He also told me I was the best he had ever seen."

Father took my hands in his. My jaws clenched involuntarily, and a chill ran up the backs of my thighs. "This is the real thing, baby," he said.

"Do you invoke a power? God or Jesus?"

"No. I never did. That's what the preachers couldn't understand. They didn't mind, though. It gave them a chance to pray and carry on—to share the glory."

I led Father to Elizabeth's bed. "Is she on her back?" he asked.

"No."

"She'll have to be."

I carefully rolled her over. Her eyes opened just long enough for her to recognize me. "Sleep," I said. And she did.

"Put my right hand on her chest," Father said, raising his eyebrows in Groucho Marx fashion. He maneuvered his hand gently, letting it come to rest below her left breast. "A shapely old gal," he said.

"Your bedside manner is a little coarse," I said.

"That's the thing about us nonmedicos. We don't have to square our conscience with any old Greek's oath. We can work on an in-bed manner."

"Not tonight, I hope."

"No." And then Father actually spit on his hands and rubbed them together. He put his right hand on Elizabeth's chest once again and said, "Here goes." His flippant manner faded. The muscles of his jaw tensed. He began to hum in soft, sustained tones. I backed away.

Elizabeth began to move her head from side to side, but she didn't open her eyes. Father sang rhythmically complex patterns of nonsense syllables. I was embarrassed and thought of covering my ears, but instead I found myself involuntarily singing. It took me a few moments to recognize what I was singing. It was part of a hymn I had learned as a child. I could not remember the name of the hymn or where I had learned it. I wondered if my singing meant that in some corner of my—my what? my soul?—I was still a Christian. My voice became louder and more confident:

> God's healing power in shadow stands
> And waits release through humblest hands.
> Repent and purify thy soul;
> Thy faith will make thy body whole.

Soon I realized that Father's chanting was not random but was forming a sort of jazz variation on my hymn. The effect was bizarre, but I no longer found it embarrassing. I looked at Elizabeth, whose head still turned from side to side. But now she moved in time to my singing. Her eyes were closed, and I wasn't sure that she was consciously hearing the hymn. Her expression was one of relaxation and delight.

Gradually, Father became silent and withdrew his

hand from Elizabeth's body. I led him to the rocking chair, and I sat opposite him, softly humming.

"I think I made some difference," Father said.

I went to the bed and touched Elizabeth's wrist. Her pulse was stronger and more regular than I had ever felt it. Keeping the fingers of my left hand on her wrist, I put the fingers of my right hand on my own wrist. My pulse and Elizabeth's were almost identical. The pulses matched the rhythm of my humming. Father was rocking to the same rhythm, but his movement gradually slowed. I led him to his bedroom, and he dropped heavily onto his bed and slept.

I returned to Elizabeth's bedside. I sang one more chorus of the hymn and, resting my head on the edge of her mattress, sank quickly into a restless semiconsciousness which was awash with unsettling images and sensations. Soon, however, I became aware of Elizabeth's hand stroking my temple. She had moved close to me, and my cheek was against her thigh. I looked up and found that she was smiling at me.

"You're reborn," I said.

"Yes, my dear."

"Through me. In my dream, I delivered you out of my body into Father's hands. Father was black. It was pleasant . . . delightful."

"Birth can only be pleasant in a dream."

"But aren't you pleased, Elizabeth? Pleased to have been reborn?"

"I see you more clearly now, my dear. My senses show you to me more vividly. That is pleasing."

"But you are also displeased."

"You're thinking I'm incapable of unalloyed happiness, that I carry about some vague discomfort as a kind of ballast."

Elizabeth was right. I had been thinking that if she couldn't be happy after a miraculous regeneration, when could she be happy?

"I always have reasons for my unhappiness, Jillian.

And I think you should sit up now and get me a towel."

Elizabeth moved to one side and pulled aside the bedclothes. On the sheet where she had been lying was a bright red stain.

"No need for alarm," Elizabeth said. "From what I recall of the process, I believe I am having my first period—is that what you call it these days?—in about twenty years."

27 | *Renascence*

Elizabeth brought a breakfast tray to my bed the next morning. She was moving quickly and surely, and her skin's old-newsprint yellowish tint had been replaced by a delicate flush. I was pleased to see her looking at ease with her body, but there was something new in her manner that displeased me. I wondered if her usual air of pride in herself had become contempt for others.

As I ate my breakfast, Elizabeth spoke, more or less to herself, and as she proceeded, it became clear that what she felt was not contempt but indignant regret.

"Eva and Shirley are demoralized," she said. "They're unkempt and sullen. Eva is one of the few people who ever inspired me. There was a summer . . . she must have been about nine. Ava was seldom in the house, and I pretended that she didn't exist . . . and she *doesn't* exist now, does she? That's what I find most despicable about David: not that he is the worthless person he is, but that he destroyed Ava. She no longer exists. He's little better than a murderer. In any case, that summer, I had decided to restore the houses's interior woodwork, which had been painted over several times. Eva was with me every moment; not scraping, staining, or varnishing, but making the most exquisite drawings of the carver's decorations. That's when she decided to become an architect, I suppose. But she made the wrong choice. Her drawings weren't architectural; they were poetic. The stylized leaf-and-vine pattern used in this room, for example, became organic in her sketches. There was a sense of life in everything she did that summer. I was the only playmate she wanted. Her father was spending the summer with a new mistress, and Eva thought he had died. She was much concerned with death—or with the denial of death. She said to me that when I died she wanted to come with me and that we could spend eternity refinishing and sketching the woodwork in heaven. That sounds sentimental to me now, but then it made me happy."

Elizabeth stood up, getting to her feet without pushing herself up with her arms as she would have had to do the day before. "I'll show you something," she said, and went into her own bedroom. She left the door open, and I watched her go to a cabinet that stood in a corner of her room. The cabinet, which was light oak, contained about two dozen shallow drawers that had probably been designed to hold sheet music. Elizabeth opened one of the drawers and pulled out several sheets of paper and brought them to me.

"These are Eva's," she said. The drawings were made in ink with an extremely fine-pointed pen on a good grade of sketch paper. Although they were competently done, the sketches didn't seem remarkable to me in any way. They showed concentration and control, but they were essentially just echoes of work done by a woodcarver. One drawing, however, was remarkable. It was a portrait of Elizabeth done quickly in simple, unshaded line. Her eyes were cast down and had the unfocused look of someone who is daydreaming. The happiness that Elizabeth had just described was obvious in the portrait. Her beauty was also clearly shown—a beauty more delicate and vulnerable than I had expected. I thought, *When I leave this house, I may not take the gold Elizabeth showed me, but I will take this drawing.* I held it out at arm's length. "You were beautiful," I said.

"I was happy. It transformed me."

"You seem happy this morning," I said.

"Not exactly. I just have more energy than yesterday. Americans seem to confuse being energetic with being happy. It's a simple enough matter to be energetic nowadays—there are pills and powders. In desperation, one can even seek out a faith healer. But I doubt whether most people are ever happy for more than a few minutes or days in a lifetime. And it's often an unexpected, unlikely combination of elements that inspires happiness. There was no particular reason I should have been even moderately joyful about my circumstances that summer. My husband had abandoned me. I believed—accurately, as it turned out—that my life would be pointless and futile. But nothing could daunt me then. There were breakfasts in the backyard when my coffee and cigarettes spiced the morning air, when Eva, in her nightdress, wandered through the damp grass, cradling a doll in her arms, when my life seemed unaccountably blessed."

Elizabeth's breathing became heavy, and her expression was rigid and trancelike. She said, "Eva and I made up a story. I had told her about the phoenix being reborn from its own ashes. She asked what would happen if there were a fireproof phoenix. In the story, a phoenix is unhappy because it has accidentally discovered that its feathers are impervious to fire. The bird will not be able to fulfill its destiny, which is to return to its birthplace a hundred years from the day of its birth to be consumed in flames and reborn from the ashes. The bird wanders throughout the world, having adventures and seeking help and advice. Finally, on its hundredth birthday, sick and dying, it returns to its birthplace. It builds a pyre and dies unscathed within the flames. It is not reborn, but instead goes to the place where dead birds go. And there, the phoenix is greatly celebrated, for, of course, it is the only bird of its kind in bird heaven. The moral was that one shouldn't be afraid to be different. We never told the story to Ava. It was our secret from her. I wondered later whether the twins had somehow fooled me and that it was unconventional Ava who had made up the story."

Elizabeth's eyelids fluttered, and I thought she might be trying to hold back tears, but she was still gazing back in time. She said, "Most of us desire something too much at some point in our lives. Some person appears, and we're willing to pay any price to have and to keep him or her. We forget that we won't live forever and that eventually we'll lose everything anyway."

I said, "Some things—for me, my father's life—are worth a sacrifice, even if you protect them only for a short time."

"Desire is the trap. Doesn't one of the Eastern religions—Buddhism or Hinduism—think our goal should be to extinguish desire?"

"Probably. But life couldn't continue without desire, could it?"

"Not earthly life, no."

"In any case, it doesn't seem as if there's much less desire being experienced in India or Japan than there is in Iowa, where we only have to worry about keeping Satan away from our souls."

"Without desire, our souls would be our own, Jillian."

"Father would say that without desire no one would have any soul."

"Your father is what we used to call a simple soul."

"But hasn't he blessed you with his simplicity?"

"I'm not sure Matthew has done me a favor. He's restored my body somewhat, but not in the way that I restored this house's woodwork to its original state. The wood retained its integrity under its paint, but my integrity—like my capacity for joy—is beyond restoration. The only pleasure I'll get from my renascence will be to watch my son's *dis*pleasure."

"He'll be here for Thanksgiving. And so will your daughter and granddaughter. It might be pleasant."

"That holiday has no relevance for my family. But I like to watch Eva and David react to each other. And I like to be with you and Matthew. The two of you offer me possibilities for pleasure or instruction. My family offers me nothing but recriminations for past failures and the lack of promise. Nevertheless, we may as well have an occasion."

"Shall I invite John Ellis?"

"Is he winning you over?"

"No. He has lost me. I was thinking Eva might enjoy his company."

"He's too young and realistic for her. But ask him. And ask young Blake for Shirley. We'll have someone for everyone but you, Jillian."

"You're for me. And I don't mind sharing you with Father."

"Maybe I *am* happy," Elizabeth said. "Maybe I can be happy in the time that is left." Elizabeth gathered up the sketches and started back to her own room. As she got to the doorway, she turned and said, "There's not *much* time left, is there?" Before I could answer, she closed the door.

28 | *To Grandmother's House*

A few days later, the Dobb family and their friends began to give thanks, and it appeared that what they were most thankful for was the gift of sexuality.

To avoid the difficulties of traveling on the Thursday of the holiday, the guests were asked to arrive for a buffet supper on Wednesday and to stay overnight. Father, Elizabeth, Eva, Shirley, and I were there to greet them.

John Ellis was the first to arrive, in late afternoon. I said hello to him from across the parlor. He looked at me questioningly, but I turned away and went to help Mary and Elizabeth in the kitchen. As I left the room, Eva appeared on the staircase, skipping down the last few steps and holding out both hands to John. She was wearing a clinging, short-skirted white dress that was so unlike her usual roomy, earth-colored outfits that there was no doubt she saw the evening as an opportunity. The dress revealed for the first time that Eva's tall figure was voluptuous, not lumpish.

Father sat in a corner of the parlor next to his cassette player and a little stack of tapes he called the Detroit collection, which consisted of tracks he had assembled featuring musicians from the Detroit area: Milt Jackson; Kenny Burrell; Sonny Stitt; Elvin, Hank, and Thad Jones; Tommy Flanagan; Pepper Adams; Donald Byrd; Paul Chambers; and Louis Hayes. The music, combined with a large bowl of hot rum-and-cider punch, quickly dissolved the guests' antagonisms and reticence.

Eva and John rolled the rug back, and they began dancing to a slow blues number. Any sense of decorum they might have intended to show deteriorated immediately into a thigh-to-thigh groping contest. Both John and Eva glanced at me occasionally—John defiantly and Eva apologetically. The glances I gave them in return were honestly fond and without resentment.

The moment Charlie Blake, the young pianist, arrived, Shirley maneuvered him into the same kind of dance-embrace that her mother was using on John. Charlie protested that he didn't know how to dance. For a few minutes, he was more interested in the music than in Shirley, and he moved toward Father, who sat at one end of the parlor, and asked questions about the musicians on the recordings. But Shirley soon gained his attention. Like her mother, she was wearing white—a soft wool pants-and-sweater outfit highlighted with a few pearl-like decorations. Although her body, unlike her mother's, was lean and angular, the two women projected the same intense sensuality. Shirley's potentially off-putting slenderness was tempered by faultless breasts and a vulnerable air.

As Eva and Shirley's success in captivating their partners became apparent, the two women began smiling at each other occasionally, and I wondered whether their performance wasn't primarily for their own benefit, a simple competition. How would they decide who was the more successful—or who would look more foolish? Their flushed faces looked scarlet in contrast with their white clothing.

I was glad I had decided to wear black.

Elizabeth, who was leaving the kitchen and putting an apron aside, was also wearing black. She had seemed to gain strength each day after her healing session with Father, and now she looked healthier—as well as vastly more serene—than her daughter.

Elizabeth went to Father and placed her mouth against his ear, apparently warning him that she was about to dance with him. She coaxed him out of his chair and drew him close to her, leading him to the dance area and guiding him smoothly around the other two couples. I doubted whether Father was pleased with the situation, but Elizabeth was obviously delighted, gathering rosebuds.

Then I felt a coldness behind me. I turned and discovered that David had arrived. He was still wearing his overcoat, which had a few melting snowflakes on it. "What kind of silliness is Mother up to?" he said.

"Hello, David. Your mother is dancing with my father."

"Where does she get the energy for that? The last time I saw her, she thought hobbling was a major accomplishment."

"Love overcomes all obstacles."

"Love is a subject I doubt that you know much about, and it's one I'm sure my mother knows nothing about." David took my arm and turned me to face him. "You underestimate her, Jillian. She's not what you think." Frown lines appeared between David's eyes. He looked frightened as well as frightening. "I'll be right back," he said, and went to put his coat in the hall closet. I wanted to push him into the closet and lock the door. An aura of destructive energy surrounded him which could create chaos in this kind of family gathering. He needed a distraction . . . a playmate. I looked around the room but saw no one who might distract him; everyone was well occupied. Apparently, the assignment was mine.

I tried to intercept David when he returned, but he bypassed me and went to speak to Elizabeth, who was still dancing—quite competently—with Father. The three of them had a short, tense conversation, and then David and Elizabeth led Father to a chair and returned together to the dance floor. Elizabeth was smiling, but David was not. I wondered about the emotions that were being generated by their little encounter. Elizabeth, who had once held the infant Ava, was now being held by the adult David. Perhaps it wasn't as unsettling for Elizabeth as I imagined. Every child eventually becomes a stranger to his or her parents, and a change from "she" to "he" is not the most unsettling change imaginable. It is no more drastic, for example, than a change from love to hate.

The music was faster now: Duke Ellington's "Cottontail" played by a rehearsal band featuring a harsh, bold baritone sax solo by Pepper Adams. Charlie Blake had led Shirley to the punchbowl, leaving Eva, John, Elizabeth, and David still dancing. Elizabeth was the most graceful and energetic of the four. David and Eva presented a strange contrast of styles: David moved awkwardly and used too much body contact; Eva was graceful but self-absorbed, as if dancing alone. John and Elizabeth both looked displeased with their partners' performances. Elizabeth, in fact, began to look extremely distressed, apparently more because of what her son was saying than because of his dancing.

I decided Elizabeth needed to be rescued, so I pried her loose from David and substituted myself for her in his arms.

"I understand your father has been creating illusions of health in my mother's failing mind," David said as he pulled me close.

"You've just had a good look at her. Is it really an illusion?"

"It has to be. I don't buy that faith-healing shit. Especially when it involves two people who couldn't work up enough faith between them to heal a hangnail."

"You should learn to accept the mysterious."

"I don't have to. I may not be your typical citizen, but my basic behavior is rational. I'm not the kind of weird person who has to drag out the supernatural to justify myself. If I decide to kill someone or to seduce someone, I'll do so for my own reasons. And if my reasons stray from the rational, they will still be human and natural."

"You should learn some humility, David."

"Have you noticed you begin every sentence with the words 'You should'?"

"I should stop doing that. Is that what you're telling me?"

David pulled me closer to him. "We could be good friends if you would do what you were told," he said. The music was slow now—a piano solo of "The Man I Love" by Tommy Flanagan. I began to feel a commonplace emotion, the kind of romantic longing described in that song. I wished the arms around me were those of someone I desired and respected; I wished the words I was hearing were devoted and arousing. Instead, I heard David say, "You're not going to do what I asked, are you?"

"Which request was that?"

David pushed me away and looked into my eyes. I remembered that he was once called Ava. "You're making a mistake, Jillian," he said. "There's not much time left. Reconsider. We could still be good friends. Uncommonly good."

I backed away from David and looked to see if Father needed anything. As I suspected, Elizabeth was taking care of his needs more than adequately. Father had a glass of punch in one hand and a slice of pizza in the other and was nodding his head and smiling at something Elizabeth was saying.

I went to the buffet table and sampled a few of the oddments the housekeeper had assembled, which were mostly crumb-covered, microwaved hors d'oeuvres that tasted alike. The punch, however, which Elizabeth had made, was warm and comforting and gave the illusion of being more nourishing than the food.

I stood alone.

Shirley was sitting in Charlie Blake's lap, and although he was paying enough attention to the music to be snapping the fingers of his right hand in time to it, his left hand moved almost imperceptibly across the cloth that covered Shirley's left breast. Her eyes were closed, she was smiling, and she nodded her head slowly, her long, straight hair moving as though on a slow-motion shampoo commercial on television.

Eva and John stood in the middle of the dance area with their hands at each other's hips. Neither was making any kind of movement that could have been interpreted as dancing. They were talking—quickly and often simultaneously—about John's house, judging from the random words I could make out. I gathered Eva might soon be making a trip to inspect it. The music stopped, and Eva and John walked toward the buffet table, still looking into each other's eyes. I turned and moved away. John wasn't even trying to conceal his rather obvious erection.

While Father was changing the tape, the room was filled with the sound of conversation. I was the wallflower. Elizabeth and Father should not have been talking to each other. I should have been with Elizabeth. It had been a mistake for Father to move into the Dobb house. I wondered whether it was a mistake for Father to accompany me on my travels. I couldn't give him the companionship I now realized he needed. He didn't have the capacity for self-sufficiency that I thought he had, and although he liked to think he was doing penance, he had the wrong kind of personality for that.

I would have to reevaluate my life. Perhaps I would even have to change in some way. But I would think about it later. Suddenly, I felt the same discomforting presence I had felt earlier. David was standing at my side, somehow still carrying with him the chill air of the late November night that lay outside the house.

What had David said to me earlier? That we could be uncommonly good friends. Was he right? We *were* both uncommon, and, like most adults, we disguised our uncommon qualities. If you had seen us at that moment, you would have thought us commonplace, two people secure in their beliefs and comfortable in their roles.

It was appropriate that David and I were paired. Certainly, I found his air of disguise and avarice more stimulating than John Ellis's cheerful lust. But I sensed that the distinctiveness that David and I shared was competitive and mutually destructive—destructive to us and to those who came too close to us. Yet there was a growing mutual fascination between us that would have to be resolved, perhaps violently.

I turned to David and looked at him invitingly, although I wasn't certain what activity I was inviting. For a moment, David's expression lacked its usual cynical quality. That was our moment of love, I thought—the moment of mutual respect that enemies occasionally allow themselves. We were two generals meeting between their armies under the flag of truce to determine if the battle is inevitable.

David produced a package of cigarettes, which he had probably borrowed from Eva. He offered me one, and I took it, even though it had been years since I had smoked. We stood at the edge of the room, staring respectfully at each other—two nonsmokers not just idly puffing but sucking the smoke in, feeling the jolt in the lungs, the quickening pulse, and the vertigo.

David glanced at his cigarette and then looked at me. "We're engaged in a lethal activity," he said.

* * *

The party was slow to end. With John and Charlie staying over, no one had to be concerned about driving, and the punchbowl was refilled several times. Each batch, under Father's direction, was more potent than the preceding one.

Shirley, who had spent the evening with one hand on Charlie Blake at all times, was the first to say good night, ascending the stairs (Charlie still in hand) to what I assumed would be a bed of bliss. Eva, not to be outdone by her daughter, then rose slowly and said, "I'll show John where his bed is."

"And which bed is that?" Elizabeth asked.

"It's the one in my room," Eva said. Her smile was impolitely self-satisfied. There were pizza-sauce stains on her white dress, and she stumbled slightly as she headed across the room. It was difficult to see this woman as either the child who had invented fairy tales or the architect who invented desirable, or at least salable, buildings.

Before David went upstairs, he kissed Elizabeth and leaned over me to brush his lips lightly across my cheek in the kind of gesture an adolescent boy might make when obliged to kiss an elderly aunt. Then he whispered, "I'll be in the attic at three A.M. I know you're too inquisitive not to join me." I shuddered and wondered whether he was right.

Elizabeth had the grace to let me lead Father up to his room. He was confused about the time, as sometimes happened when he had been drinking heavily—confused not about the hour or day but about the decade. It would be to Elizabeth's benefit, I thought. Judging from his mutterings, he was imagining himself as he was in his mid-thirties.

I left Father and went to my own room. I wasn't ready to sleep, and I felt abandoned. I lay on the bed and let images drift through my consciousness. I remembered Thanksgiving days I had spent as a child in my grandmother's house . . . over the river and through the woods. It occurred to me for the first time that the words of the old song specified that we go to grandmother's house, not to grandfather's.

Grandmother had raised me. I tried to recall whether in sociology classes we were told that American society had become a matriarchy. It seemed that way to me. From the time of my childhood, the men in my experience were elusive, impermanent figures. They weren't necessarily weak, but they didn't make strong, permanent human connections. Since the women's movement of the 1960s and 1970s, the influence of women had been extended and strengthened. For many women, such as Ava/David Dobb, who shared men's values, the progress hadn't been good enough. But I have my own values. I think there is a peculiarly female relationship to life. It is we who give birth, who have a special closeness to the bringing forth of life. Perhaps some of us also have a special relationship to death. Were there other women who, like me, had not brought forth souls in birth but had sent forth souls in death? Were there others who saw death not, as men tended to, as an ending but as a renewal? Christians, as well as members of other religions, spoke of being reborn through death, but theirs was a passive belief. My belief was active.

I supposed some people might say that I had developed some kind of emotional quirk because of being raised by my grandmother, that I was the victim of a psychological or emotional aberration. But they would underrate me and others of my kind—the kind who are not content to feed their lives on doses of brightly colored soap opera or to devise degrading career plans that will take them into fluorescent-lit corporate boardrooms. We are the kind who face the shadows and who seek a more venerable, more esoteric approach to life.

I knew I couldn't sleep. I went downstairs, where Elizabeth was collecting some of the debris of the party. Although I knew she had drunk her share of punch, she seemed less affected by it than any of the rest of us. I kissed her. "Go upstairs," I said. "I'll clean things up."

"I feel too young," she said. "It's unsettling. I liked the feeling of being at the edge of the precipice." Elizabeth returned my kiss. "You'll take me back to the edge, won't you?"

"If you'd like."

"And beyond?"

"Eventually."

"Bless you."

Elizabeth went to her bed of joy and pain. I wandered amid the dross and rubbish of the party, looking for dangers such as smoldering cigarettes, or offenses to the housekeeper such as mashed food on the furniture.

Eventually, I returned to my room. It was not a quiet night. First there were the flushings and sloshings of the house's antique plumbing. Then there were thumpings and creakings, and voices—voices of encouragement, warning, satisfaction, appreciation, and, I imagined, apology. The sounds became less frequent and less clamorous. I began to doze. And then, just before three o'clock, I heard a door open and someone—David, presumably—climbing the narrow, uncarpeted stairway to the attic. I rose immediately and followed him. I realized I had been waiting for this all evening.

29 | *Someone's in the Attic with David*

The attic seemed darker than it had on my first visit, and it was colder. In the dim, bluish light, the heaps of trash created a surface that would have looked more appropriate on another planet. I couldn't see or hear David, but he had to know I was there because I had closed the door loudly behind me when I entered.

I stood quietly and moved my head slowly from side to side, waiting to see movement or to recognize David's figure. I felt like a scanning camera on the moon, except that I was experiencing some human but ambiguous emotions. The emotions began to clarify and change when I finally caught sight of David. Curiosity became amusement, which in turn became distaste. David had been lying motionless amid the stack of women's clothing at the top of one of the piles of discarded material. He was wearing a floor-length woman's robe made of a light-colored translucent material. He stood up awkwardly and gained his footing long enough to strike a showgirl pose, with one arm akimbo and the other raised slightly above his head. He lost his balance almost immediately, though, and sank to his knees.

David looked in my direction and said, "I'm out of practice, my dear. And I don't usually have an audience." He giggled and rolled slowly down the side of the mound, holding a few crumpled garments in each hand. When he reached the floor, he stood up and held a short red dress against his body. "This is where

189

I commune with my former self." David waited for me to speak, but I had no idea what to say. "What's in Jillian's mind?" he continued. "Is Jillian disapproving? I have no idea how I affect you, my dear. In fact, I have no idea how anything on this earth affects you. I can't decide whether you're some kind of bizarre saint or whether you're simply a psychopath."

David dropped the red dress and walked toward me, stepping carefully with his bare feet among the discarded objects. "It's unlike you to be speechless," he said. He was right; I was literally unable to speak. "I'll ask you questions you can nod yes or no to, shall I?"

I nodded yes.

"Are you frightened?"

No.

"I don't know why not. Are you sexually aroused?"

No.

"Again, I don't know why not. You're certainly the only one in the house tonight who isn't. Will this help?" David opened his robe and walked toward me. His chest was glossy and hairless but flat and muscular. The plasticized effect of his skin ended below his rib cage. Below his navel began a luxuriant growth of auburn pubic hair that seemed to end in the standard female pudenda. Visible through the hair of his abdomen were the pale lines of surgical incisions and the cross-hatching of stitches.

"Still not aroused?"

No.

"But at least I've satisfied your curiosity. Would you like to touch?"

No.

"Did I sense a little hesitation?"

No. No.

David moved quickly to within reach of me. He took my hand and pressed it quickly between his legs.

I pulled away, but not before getting the sense of a conventional vulval arrangement.

"Now you know," David said, and tied his robe closed. "But you don't want to know more, do you?"

No.

"May I hold you?"

I wanted to shake my head no once more, but it didn't move. David put his arms around me. I crossed my arms over my chest as a barrier, but I didn't push him away.

"What am I going to do with you, Jillian? You won't attend to my mother. You spurn my affection. You're an impediment. On the other hand, you *are* in the attic *and* in my arms. You can't think I'm all bad." Keeping me in his arms, David moved around in back of me. He whispered in my ear, "I could become angry—desperately angry. I could, so to speak, take things into my own hands." He put his hands on my neck and applied pressure—enough pressure to make me realize he was unusually strong, and enough to make me instinctively reach up to pull his hands away. He quickly lowered his hands and placed his fingers under the front of my bra. "And what's this?" he said. He held the snapshot of Elizabeth and her friends that I had tucked away earlier.

"How sweet," he said. "Your idea of a pinup . . . lesbians on the loose. I can't compete with that. But it does send me into a rage of jealousy." Quickly, he tore the picture in half.

I found my voice, and it trembled with anger. "You're a monster," I said. I wasn't sure why I reacted so violently to the tearing up of the photograph, but it seemed extremely important that I get it back, as if it were the only picture I had of some particularly close relatives. I reached for the photograph, but David held it away from me. I felt like a schoolgirl being teased by the class bully. I reached once more for the torn picture, my body pressing against David's. "Please," I said. It was the schoolgirl's plea. Next he would expect tears. Once again, David began to maul me and to ask for sexual favors, all of which repelled me. I wondered why I had thought earlier that we might form some kind of bond.

David eventually gave up the struggle. He handed me the torn photograph and said, "Have you ever in your life just relaxed and let someone take a few hours to discover what might give you full sexual pleasure?"

I saw no reason to answer him, but the answer would have been no.

"You have to be in charge of the encounter to get any sexual pleasure, don't you?"

"In charge or not, I couldn't get any pleasure from an encounter with a monster."

"You don't mate with your own species, then?"

"I am not a monster."

"Some might say you are. Some of your actions are certainly monstrous."

"My actions are not monstrous. They grow out of mutual human needs. They're developed respectfully."

"I have human needs, too, my dear. Right now, I need to watch you take your black dress off. I need to see your breasts. What could be more human? If you were so respectful, you would—"

I interrupted. "Pig. You're a pig."

"I've dropped in your esteem. I'm just a pig now. A minute ago, I was a monster. I prefer 'monster,' I think. That's closer to it, I believe."

I nodded. My voice had failed again.

David continued. "We're not going to be friends. I can finally see that. But you'll regret that. And you'll regret it soon, Jillian."

I turned and fled to my room. David was right in

thinking that one of us would soon find cause for regret. I had always assumed he would be the regretful one—the loser—but now I felt some doubt. The initiative was with David. I was retreating. And the rest of the night I lay in fear and confusion, surrounded by lovers.

30 | *We Give Thanks*

I left my bed gratefully at dawn. The housekeeper had asked me to transfer the turkey from the refrigerator to a low-heat oven. On the way down to the kitchen, I glanced into Elizabeth's room and was relieved to see that she was alone in her bed.

I went to my room and stood at the window, waiting for full light. I wished it were a clear day in June with early, brilliant sunlight. I thought of John Ellis, who spent so much of his time standing in the warmth and clarity of direct sun. He should not be among us, I thought. He was a bird among cats. He had followed me not because of what he thought I might have done to his mother but because I was the same kind of person his mother was. She and I saw the night as a time of somber transactions, while John saw the night as a setting for physical pleasure. For John, darkness was merely an exotic type of light instead of a manifestation of truths he had recognized as a child but had long ago forgotten. He, like so many in this age, is blinded by the light.

Yet there are times when all of us need the light—times like that Thanksgiving morning, when I knew that the darkness was about to release its powers. That dinner was the eye of the storm. The sun appeared, and those who were blessed with simple souls prepared to offer thanks for their blessings.

I prepared for the night that would follow, a night for which no one would be thankful.

The dining room faced south, and a slanting afternoon sunlight filled the room. Elizabeth sat at the head of the table facing David. The rest of us were spectators on the sidelines. Eva and Shirley were undone by romance—Eva thoughtfully and Shirley mindlessly. Afraid that someone would dispel her rapture, Eva stood up as soon as the wine glasses were filled. She said, "There was a time—when this house was new—that grace would have been spoken at this point."

I looked at Elizabeth, who was being indirectly accused of godlessness by her daughter. Elizabeth's eyebrows were raised slightly, but she seemed placid.

Eva continued. "Concepts of grace change, but I think we all agree that there are moments in life when we feel blessed, when we want to express our gratitude for life's favors."

"Favors such as a good lay," David muttered. He was sitting next to me, and I think I was only one who heard what he said. But everyone heard the enormous sigh he heaved after the remark. Elizabeth was staring tolerantly at her plate. Charlie looked puzzled. Shirley was looking fondly at her mother and nodding in agreement. Father looked amused, and John was wearing a ridiculous expression of modest pride.

Eva ignored her brother. "I think," she said, "it would be appropriate if each of us recalled something . . . some incident that made us grateful."

I did a quick survey of the expressions around the table. There were two types: indifferent and distressed.

Eva was undeterred. "I think we should start with Mr. Cole . . . Matthew, can you recall something for us? Just some small thing. A precious moment."

Poor Father. How would he react? I was sure he

realized, as I did, that his response would set the tone for the rest of the dinner. I hoped he would either change the subject or say something silly. Instead, he seemed to be taking the suggestion seriously.

"Looking for wisdom, are you? Young people think that a person who's been fucked over enough will come out of it being wise. But the only thing old people get is old, and the last thing young people are interested in is wisdom."

David perked up. He said, "The last thing *anyone* is interested in is wisdom. The only thing anyone is interested in, or grateful for, is feeling good."

"Well, I can remember feeling good once or twice," Father said. "Here's one . . ."

It will be about music or sex, I thought.

"I went for a walk one misty morning in the Blue Ridge Mountains, and I knew it was either spring or fall, but I didn't know which one . . ."

The others looked a little puzzled, but I was touched. He was remembering how that morning looked, remembering what it was like to see something beautiful.

"The sun was low and pale; everything soft-edged and black, white, or gray; no leaves. I couldn't remember the season."

"And what was there to be grateful for?" David asked. "Your confusion?"

"Right," Father said. "Absolutely right. That was the lesson: things are more beautiful if you're confused. It's like hearing a piano player start to play a tune, and you're not sure what the meter is or where the bar lines would be drawn. Beautiful."

David said, "I've always had trouble knowing where to draw the line, but I've never been burdened by a sense of beauty."

I was sure David was being honest. It would explain something about his coldness. I thought of asking him to say more about beauty, but I didn't want to offend

Eva by interrupting her game. However, she had slumped down in her chair and was no longer trying to be the director of activities; she was pale and breathing heavily, her body probably having decided it had encountered too much alcohol.

I thought the gratefulness game had been abandoned, but Elizabeth said, "There was a Sunday afternoon in Rome . . . actually, a noon, not an afternoon . . . we were in a public garden . . . a park above the city, and the bells of the churches began to ring . . . thousands of bells, thousands of pitches and patterns. I could smell flowers and pine needles. It was the only time I had a sense of a god—not the god of the Italians, with their singing and strong coffee, but the gods of the ancient Romans, who slept in their capes on the frontiers of their empire. It was the moment I began to understand that I had a pagan streak in me."

Was Elizabeth still a pagan? It seemed to me that of the people at the table, she was the one most likely to believe in something in the religious sense. Did she believe in Venus and Diana? Was there a sibyl that she consulted?

The game seemed to be taking hold. Everyone was tinkering with wine glasses or plates, but they seemed to be searching their memories for moments that matched those described by Father and Elizabeth. Eva and Shirley were smiling to themselves, Charlie looked pleasantly puzzled, David looked thoughtful, and John seemed to have tears in his eyes.

John cleared his throat.

He'll say something conventional, I thought.

But he said, "What changed my life was picking up a major-league baseball bat for the first time. White hickory with a dark grain. Louisville Slugger. It was like a holy object."

David said, too loudly, "A phallic object, more likely."

197

John sneered at David, but the sneer was not too effective because of his tears. If Eva hadn't been sitting between John and David, something violent might have happened. Instead, John pulled a handkerchief out of his pocket and blew his nose.

Eva, after also sneering at her brother, spoke predictably—but not convincingly, I thought—about a building. "The sight I'm most grateful for is the Abbey Church of St. Philibert at Tournus, in France."

David muttered something about name-dropping.

"I won't try to describe it for you," Eva continued, "but the little grove of pillars that greets you in its narthex has an unearthly effect."

I didn't know what Eva was talking about, and I supposed no one else did either. Whether David understood his sister or not, he wasn't ready to give up his theme. "I suppose," he said, "that pillars—especially en grove—are more seriously phallic than a simple baseball bat." He seemed to have taken over direction of the gratitude game. "Jillian," he said, "I'm sure you can come up with—so to speak—something more arresting than sexual symbols."

His use of the word *arresting* was not accidental, but I wasn't accepting any challenges. I hadn't taken Eva's game seriously at first, but now I could see, through the windows facing me, the darkness developing outside, and I thought of death—the dying day, the dying year. David was squandering his life, I thought, and resented the sense of life—odd and tentative though it was—that had developed during the dinner. I would try to treat the game with respect; I would try to describe a moment for which I was truly grateful.

What in my life had gratified me? The years before I became a companion seemed vague and dull to me, like years spent in a chrysalis. I remembered Elizabeth's "Poor Butterfly." But in my case, it wasn't the butterfly/companion who was to be pitied, but the wormlike creature I once had been. There must have been a moment at which the metamorphosis had taken place for me. As the people around the table looked toward me expectantly, I remembered the only night in my adult life that I had prayed: the night when my father was in the hospital after his injury. The doctors thought he might become comatose, might never recover consciousness. I had thought of going to one of the churches that Father occasionally worked in—mostly storefronts or abandoned big-denomination buildings—but it was just after midnight in the middle of the week, and those places would be locked up. I left the hospital and began to walk. Then it occurred to me that if Father hadn't been in the hospital, he would have been at a jazz club. The old El Sino was near the hospital, and I went there.

It was a cool, rainy spring night, and only a few people were in the club. A local group was playing—a quartet made up of a young alto saxophonist and a rhythm section. They were playing an extended version of "I'll Be Seeing You," an ironic title but a beautifully mournful melody. I wept. Father would never again be seeing me. That was beyond question. But the doctors said he might escape brain damage. He might still be able to listen to the music he loved. I prayed for that. I would have given my life for that. And before I left the club, I somehow knew that my prayer would be answered.

"Well, my dear?" David said. "Sorting through your countless gratifying moments?"

"Remembering one. The night I prayed in a nightclub while someone played 'I'll Be Seeing You.'"

Father grinned. I had told him the story several times. His response was always the same: "That's a nice tune, 'I'll Be Seeing You.' Billie Holiday liked it." And he would embrace me.

But now, he just said, "I owe you one, sweetie."

Charlie Blake, who had been looking uncomfortable through the recitations, proved his musical kin-ship with Father by saying, " 'I'll Be Seeing You' has a nice structure . . . and the thing I was grateful for was the first time I reached a tenth with my left hand. For a while, I thought my hands were going to be too small for that."

Shirley Dobb took one of Charlie's hands, which did look small for a pianist's. Charlie's embarrass-ment at having had to make a sentimental statement was replaced by a new embarrassment over Shirley's show of affection.

Shirley looked across the table at her mother. The look combined affection and schoolgirl silliness. "I don't know if this is the sort of thing you're supposed to say," Shirley murmured. "But one of the happy moments I can remember is"—she lowered her eyes —"being nursed by you, Mom. I can remember it as clearly as I can remember anything."

Eva's reaction was ambiguous, as if she wanted to be pleased by what she heard but was not able to manage it.

Shirley wasn't to be dissuaded, though. "It was just one time that I remember. You had on a blue-and-white checked blouse. You unbuttoned it and moved it away from your breast—your left breast. It was beautiful."

I looked at John Ellis, who was smiling. He was probably thinking that the anatomical feature in question still had its charms. The rest of us, with one exception, seemed relieved that the game was almost over. The one exception was the person who hadn't yet recited: David. He seemed furious, and I thought I knew why. Eva's breasts (which, as clearly indicated by her clinging blouse, were still formidable) were probably about as emotionally explosive as any topic could be for David, considering the history of his body. They were a feature he had chosen not to have. Eva, Elizabeth, Father, and I, knowing his secret, understood his fury. But the person he turned that fury on—Shirley—was unprepared for his reaction. "You disgusting creature," he said to her venomously.

It wasn't a popular remark. Shirley looked shocked and tearful. Charlie said, defensively, "Hey, man."

But Elizabeth asserted her authority as the head of the family. "Now, David," she said. "I know that the various aspects of motherhood offend you, but remember why we're here. You get the last word, which you've always been good at."

Eva added, "But it has to be about gratitude, which our David has *never* been good at." Eva sat up straight, and her shoulders were pulled back.

David surrendered not by apologizing but by sighing and shrugging. His life was not easy, I thought, and I felt a little pang of sympathy for him. I wondered why I sympathized more readily with people who brought on their own difficulties than I did with those who were innocent. I understood David's emotions better than I did Shirley's.

"It's true," David said. "I am a stranger to gratitude. There are two problems. First, I have had very little to be grateful for; and second, even when I have felt grateful, I haven't known whom to thank."

"You could thank your grammar teacher," Elizabeth said.

"That's you, I suppose," David replied.

Elizabeth said, "I'll take some of the credit."

"Then that's the moment I'm grateful for," David said. "The moment I mastered the subtleties of case and pronoun."

No one looked amused. The others were probably wondering, as I was, whether David truly felt no gratitude for the events of his life. Did he think that his grand transsexual experiment had been a failure? Had he begun to regret that no child would ever feed at his breast?

No. What he said next revealed that it was nothing

as simple as that. "I'm saving my thankfulness," David said. "As we all should. For the time may come for you, as it soon will come for me, when you will have cause for enormous gratitude—when you'll have to draw on your reserves." David raised his glass to Elizabeth and said, "Here's to future causes for thanksgiving."

The game had ended.

31 | *A Soul Departs*

Despite the tensions at the dinner table, the meal concluded with general contentment. Elizabeth had made a dessert that was traditional in her family: a cross between pumpkin pie and Indian pudding with a base of pumpkin, apple, corn meal, and molasses baked in a lattice-top pie crust and served warm with whipped cream. We all said we were too full to do justice to it, but everyone managed to eat at least a small helping.

When the last person had finished eating, Elizabeth stood up. "I think I'll go for a drive," she said. There was a moment of confusion as food-and-drink-befuddled minds tried to understand her. Elizabeth didn't own a car and hadn't driven in years. Had she had a relapse of some kind and lost the vigor and clearness of mind that she had shown since the healing session with Father? Was this an episode of senility—had her memory slipped back three or four decades?

"Do you want me to drive you?" David asked.

"I'll drive myself," Elizabeth said. "Whose car is the biggest? I'm used to a big car."

"That's mine, I guess," John said. The battered station wagon he had driven me to Chicago in was outside.

"Is there anything exotic about its controls?" Elizabeth asked.

"No," John said, "unless you consider a gear shift exotic." He was obviously displeased about the possibility of either Elizabeth or the station wagon coming to harm.

"There's no need for you to drive, Elizabeth," I said. "I can do that for you." I wondered if there was any need for her to go out at all. The effects of Father's healing had been dramatic, but I assumed they were imaginary and temporary. Elizabeth could easily overtax her heart. But as she stood up, she seemed strong as well as determined, and I was inquisitive about her purpose in leaving the house. We put on jackets, and after borrowing keys from an obviously displeased John, we went to his car. Although I had no uncertainty about my driving ability, I was a little uneasy about driving without the license I had discarded years ago. As we drove out of town, the sun was low, and the day's wintry brightness was converting quickly and garishly into darkness. Alternate bands of bluish-orange and black stretched across the southwestern horizon. I switched the headlights on.

"There's no pleasure in driving after sunset," Elizabeth said. "But I want to be alone with you."

I drove us to the spot that John had taken me to the other night. I shut off the engine, and we unbuckled our seat belts. Cold and silence surrounded us.

"Lovers' Lane," I said.

"I know."

I waited for Elizabeth to say something else. I was content just to be with her in the growing darkness, to be with my companion. I moved closer to her. She said, "I shall miss you, Jillian."

I began to feel uncomfortably cold. "What do you mean? Do you want me to leave?"

"No. I am the one who will leave you."

Was Elizabeth asking my help in taking her leave? My help was something we had never discussed explicitly. With her, as with most of my companions, such a discussion hadn't seemed necessary. My assistance—the performance of my final duties—was understood. It was something that would happen naturally, in its own time. But the time didn't seem to be right for Elizabeth. "I thought you'd been happier lately, more committed to life," I said.

"That's true. My departure has nothing to do with my wishes. Or with yours, Jillian. David is going to kill me."

A spasm moved quickly through my body.

"Are you all right, Jillian?" Elizabeth asked. "I didn't mean to shock you. I thought you knew."

"You used a word I don't like."

"Kill? Yes. It's unpleasant. But it's true."

"How can you know it's true?"

"David told me . . . and lying is not one of his vices."

"He specializes in the major vices, then."

"In some of them, yes."

"And why will he take your life?"

"Because of you, Jillian."

Elizabeth seemed determined to shock me. "I don't understand," I said.

"David believes that if I were to be murdered when you were in the house, the authorities would never believe that anyone but you could be guilty. You are his license to kill me, he says."

Good old David.

Elizabeth continued. "Is David correct about you?"

"Even assuming he is, why would he want to kill you?"

"For two compelling reasons: he hates me, and he wants my money."

"I suspect his greed is stronger than his hate. Can't you simply cut him out of your will? That would destroy half—the stronger half—of his motive."

"I thought I had taken care of that years ago. My will specifies that David can inherit only if it is established that he was not responsible for my death in any way."

I was David's alibi. The situation had become ludicrous. There was only one thing for me to do. I took Elizabeth's hand and said, "Father and I will leave tomorrow."

"Is that the only way?"

"I think so."

We had both begun to shiver. I started the engine and turned on the heater.

Elizabeth said, "How many have there been?"

I didn't answer.

"All of them, Jillian? All six?"

"I thought you knew."

"How would I know, my dear?"

"The picture," I said. "The snapshot. You were all there. I thought it was something magical, inexplicable."

The snapshot was at the house, in my room, its two pieces rejoined by transparent tape.

"I don't know about the snapshot," Elizabeth said. "I can't imagine what it is. But I'm sure it's not magical. Nothing in my life had been magical until you and your father entered it."

We listened to the sounds of the engine and the heater. I felt tears begin to form. Elizabeth's hand tightened on mine, and she said, "I want you to proceed, Jillian. Tonight. Proceed with what you had planned to do to me . . . to do *for* me."

Before I could answer, there was another shock to my system.

There was a sharp rapping on the trunk of the car, and a light appeared in the back window. The light moved slowly around to the driver's window. I rolled the window down. The light went out, allowing us to make out the form of a police officer. It was Jay Barnett. He gave no indication that he recognized me.

He did recognize Elizabeth, however. He said, "Mrs. Dobb?"

She didn't speak.

"I'm Officer Barnett. I'm glad to see you out and about. But this isn't the safest place to be after dark."

"Yes. Thank you," Elizabeth said.

I no longer felt chilled. My cheeks were particularly warm.

Jay looked at me and smiled with what seemed to be professional insincerity. "I'm sure you have your driver's license, Miss," he said, "so I won't ask to see it. Drive safely getting home. Good night, ladies."

I wondered if I would ever see him again. I almost said *Ja, Ja,* to him.

Elizabeth and I drove back in silence, and I thought about her request. Somehow it seemed immoral.

When we returned to the house, there was an air of what I assumed to be lethargy, but I might have seen it as menace if I had been more alert. John and Charlie were watching a football game on television, and Father was with them, complaining about the irrelevance of the broadcasters' comments. Shirley and Eva were in the kitchen. David was not in sight. I wondered whether he was in the attic.

The atmosphere of romance seemed to have dissipated, probably as a result of the heavy meal. Father had once told me, "To get rid of an unwanted attack of randiness, eat a big plate of food."

Elizabeth went upstairs, and I went to a corner of the parlor. I wanted to think about what she had said in the car. But there wasn't much chance for thinking, for I seemed to have become a minor center of attention. One by one, four visitors stopped by to talk to me briefly. In the cases of Charlie Blake and John Ellis, the visits were goodbyes.

Charlie's visit was especially moving. He was not

fond of, or good at, talking, and it took a few minutes before I realized that what he was trying to tell me was how much he admired my father. The words of Charlie's I remember are, "I thought if you were old you had to be bogus. Don't take him away."

Shirley's conversation wasn't much more direct than Charlie's. Her admiration was for me. "You didn't settle for all that conventional shit," she said. "You know things that not everybody knows. Maybe you'll teach me sometime."

Eva thanked me for having restored her mother's interest in life. Eva was also grateful that I had introduced her to John, who had restored some of her own interests. She was trying to apologize to me for having confiscated John's affections. She announced that she was going into the business of restoring houses, using John's home as her headquarters. She and Shirley had packed while Elizabeth and I were out, and they would be leaving with John in a few minutes.

John said I would never have learned to like baseball. That was true, but what he didn't realize was that the reason I would not have been able to live with him was that he used oversimplifications of that kind in the few attempts he made to understand his life. He also said that he thought his mother had loved me. He was almost right.

After John talked to me, my four visitors made a few trips upstairs to bring down luggage and boxes of belongings. They had said goodbye to David and Elizabeth. Father and I went out onto the porch and waved. In the twentieth-century fashion, our last memory of our friends was the sight (for Father, the sound) of their cars turning a corner. Father and I sat down together on the sofa, and he fell asleep in my arms.

About an hour later, I heard a terrifying sound from

upstairs. My first thought was that an animal was trapped in the attic. But the only animals in the house were humans. And humans only make such sounds when they are in extreme distress. I made Father comfortable on the sofa, and I went upstairs to Elizabeth's room.

Elizabeth lay on her bed, her eyes bulging, her tongue swollen and extended, and her face blotched in scarlet. Her chest was rising and falling rapidly, and there was a horrible, hacking sound in her throat. Someone—it could only have been David—had tried to strangle her. He had done a clumsy job, disfiguring his mother unnecessarily.

I kissed Elizabeth's forehead and knelt at the side of the bed. She seemed to recognize me, but she was obviously in great pain. The time had come, as it had come with all my companions, when I was being silently entreated to end the suffering that others had caused. Few of us, at the end, will avoid suffering and despair; few will not wish for a compassionate, resolute companion to bring them peace.

I wanted Elizabeth to speak. I couldn't remember what words she had last said to me. I looked into her eyes to see if there was a message. I wanted at least to see an expression that was the equivalent of her surprising, formal conversation. But I saw only pain. I would bring David's act to completion, but it would remain his responsibility. He was the killer.

I leaned over my dear Elizabeth, and as my tears dropped onto my hands, I quickly brought her the peace she craved. I lowered her eyelids and kissed them.

And so, when the moment came, after all the discussion and anticipation, it was terrifyingly simple. Here was the reason for all the prohibitions against the taking of life. It is a simple, absolute act to which there is no adequate response. And the ultimate consequences of the act—for either the victim or the one who commits the act—are unknown.

Added to the simplicity and mystery of the act is our knowledge that we are all subject to it.

As I turned away from the bed, my hand touched a book that was half hidden in the bedclothes. It was *Jane Eyre*. The book was opened to the last page of the text. It described the imminent death of Jane's former friend St John Rivers.

A few words were underlined. I read them aloud: "And why weep for this? No fear of death will darken St John's last hour; his mind will be unclouded, his heart will be undaunted, his hope will be sure, his faith steadfast."

From behind me, a voice said, "How touching." It was David. "Touching," he said, "but inappropriate." He was standing in the shadows, and his voice was strained. "I asked you to reconsider," he said. "I obviously botched the job. It would have been better for her in every way if you had done it. And you might as well have done it, because I can guarantee that you will be blamed for it . . . blamed, but not necessarily punished. I'll give you until morning—six o'clock— to leave town. There's a bus then. I'll call the police at seven and tell them what you've done—what you've done to Elizabeth tonight and to others in the past. They'll be delighted. Network TV news. Serial murderer."

"Leave me alone with her," I said.

For the next half-hour, I stayed on my knees beside Elizabeth's bed. Where was her soul? Was it irretrievably lost?

Perhaps not. It could be that David had stolen it. But I could retrieve it from him.

32 | *Retribution*

I walked slowly down the stairway, my vision obscured by tears. Father was still asleep on the sofa. I sat next to him and woke him by taking his arms and placing them around my shoulders. I rested my head on his chest and cried silently.

Father eventually said, "Is Elizabeth dead?"

"Yes."

"David did it?"

"Yes."

"She told me it was going to happen."

"She was right. And it means I have to leave in the morning."

"I'm always ready, sweetie."

"I'm going alone."

"And what's going to become of dear old Dad?"

"You could be happy here. I'll take you to your room at Mrs. Tickle's place. She'll care for you. John Ellis and Eva won't be far away, and Charlie Blake will be even closer. They all love you."

"Doesn't Jillian love me?"

I began to sob.

"I'm sorry, Jillian. That was a dumb question."

"I've done things you don't know about . . . things you might have wondered about or guessed. I don't have time now to explain them. They're things I have to atone for. You know about that. And leaving you is part of the atonement."

"Sweetie, I know about you . . . I know all about

you. And one of the things I know is that you're a little out of gear now. I want to go up and be with Elizabeth a little bit, and I want you to rest."

We went cautiously up the stairs and into Elizabeth's bedroom. I closed the door behind us. Elizabeth looked even more ghastly than she had before. The blotches on her face and neck stood out more lividly against a grayish pallor. I was glad Father didn't have to see her. "I should cover her," I said. "But I can't touch her; I can't even walk toward her."

"I can," Father said. When he entered the room, he had put his hand against the foot of her bed to orient himself. He moved around to the side of the bed, running his hand lightly up Elizabeth's body. His hand paused at her throat and then quickly moved away. He picked up a light blanket that had been folded at the foot of the bed and, after holding Elizabeth's head for a minute, spread the blanket carefully over the body. I wondered if he was remembering what it was like to cry.

"Elizabeth was a good old gal," he said.

"But David is *not* good."

"No. David's a villain."

"I have to talk to him before I leave," I said.

"Before *we* leave," Father said. "You and I will have some quiet years together."

I took Father to his room and let him start gathering his belongings. I went, as I knew I must, but without enthusiasm, to find the villain.

I moved into the hallway with the awkward slowness of a drugged person. The drug was fear. The air seemed cold as it reached my lungs, and each breath was a little shock. I stood in the hallway and listened for a sound that might indicate where David was, but the only sounds came from Father's room.

My fear grew out of uncertainty. What would happen when I found David? I was seeking retribution, but did I have the strength to gain it? David was strong, and he was in a state of turmoil. I would have to soothe and distract him. I needed a strategy. I decided to postpone my visit to his room.

I went to my bedroom and stood confused in the semidarkness. I was facing the full-length mirror of a massive old wardrobe. I hadn't given much thought to my appearance lately. I was pale and disheveled. I looked like a victim, and I didn't want David to see me in that condition. I opened the wardrobe and looked at my meager, shabby collection of clothes. There was nothing that would catch David's attention.

At least, I thought, I could clean myself up. I went into the bathroom and began to fill the tub. I went back to my bedroom and took off my clothes. David liked to watch women disrobe. Perhaps that was the way to pacify him. But an effective strip tease requires interesting and elaborate undergarments; mine were utilitarian. I went to Elizabeth's room, and, being careful not to look in the direction of her bed, I quickly went through closets and drawers, uncovering scores of extravagant old undergarments, night-dresses, and robes. I put together an ensemble, knowing that the fit would not be perfect, but hoping I would at least be able to get into everything.

After bathing, I dressed in Elizabeth's things, which fit reasonably well. The bra was a bit snug, but I didn't think David would find that unappealing. Then I recalled the white tunic I had worn on the night John Ellis's mother had died. I went to my room and put it on over the lingerie. I thought David would be pleased by its virginal simplicity. I felt like an acolyte about to take part in a secret ceremony.

I put on a pale-blue silk robe over the tunic. I paused to look at myself in the full-length mirror. My face was taking on color, and its flush contrasted subtly with the white of the tunic, the blue of the open robe, and the darkness of my loose hair. I went more confidently to David's room. In the pocket of my robe, I had put the waist ties of four other robes.

I opened the door of David's bedroom without knocking. He was sitting on his bed with his back against the headboard. The room was fogged with cigarette smoke, and an open bottle of scotch was on the bedside table.

He didn't seem surprised to see me. "I found an old—a *very* old—pack of cigarettes," he said. "Unfiltered. The kind for truly suicidal personalities . . . maybe you'd like one."

I shook my head.

"What is it you *do* want? Did you come to chastise me?"

"I suppose I wanted to give you a chance to explain yourself . . . to justify yourself."

"I couldn't possibly explain myself in the time you have available, and I see no need to justify myself." David reached for the bottle of scotch. "Will you at least have some of this?" he asked. "There's a glass in the bathroom. I've been going directly to the source." He took a substantial swig from the bottle, which was nearly empty.

I thought it likely that David wasn't too drunk to walk. I got the glass from the bathroom and poured some whiskey into it. I sat on the bed and sipped the whiskey gratefully. "Did you hate your mother?" I asked. "Or were you just desperate to get her money?"

"Despised her. She tried to drown me when I was a little girl."

I saw no point in trying to get David to make sense. I would just let him babble, which is what he did between puffs on a series of cigarettes and gulps from the bottle. "These are old-fashioned drugs," he said. "Everything here is old—which would have been all right if she had given me some fucking money. People don't realize what a serious matter stinginess is. What good is her money doing her now?" David looked thoughtful for a moment. "She took things well at the end. She'd always been com- . . . comfortable with death, even her own. She sent her farewells to you and Eva. It was always the ladies that interested her."

Speech was becoming more difficult for him. "What's all this about the phoenix, though? She asked for a little reprieve . . . I expected a prayer . . . but she told a story . . . a children's story . . . sun on the morning grass . . . Mother with Eva and me in her arms . . . ascending, she said . . . we would find our heaven . . . we would be celebrated . . ."

David lit a new cigarette from the one he held. "We'll see her in hell, won't we, Jillian?"

"Not you, David. You're not good enough."

"I thought—as Mae West said—goodness had nothing to do with it."

"You've served only yourself, David. Selfishness is beyond good and evil. In the end, you will turn in on yourself and vanish in your own emptiness."

"A universal black hole for a soul."

David tilted the whiskey bottle again. He seemed on the verge of dropping into unconsciousness. I held out my glass, and he refilled it awkwardly. I waited. He began to make a vaguely songlike sound, and his eyes opened and closed in a pattern that resembled slow-motion blinking. Eventually, his eyes stopped opening. I took the bottle and his cigarette from him. Then he made a little series of disgusting, constricted snores. The snoring was so violent that I thought he might be going to choke to death and that I would only have to stand and watch. But even though the violence of his breathing didn't decrease, it became plain he was in no danger.

I slowly lowered David in the bed and spread-eagled him on his back. I took out the four robe belts that were in my pocket. They were of varied materials— one of them was a plaited cord—but they all seemed strong. The bed was decorated at the head and foot with heavy, fluted posts. I tied David's feet to the lower corner posts, and then, more carefully, began to tie his wrists to the top corners. I didn't know anything about knot tying, and I simply made a series of random loopings. I knew I had to pull the bonds tightly around his wrists, and, as I feared, he opened his eyes as I tightened the first one. He was alert almost immediately, and he grabbed my arm with his free hand. "Bitch," he said. He looked at the bindings on his wrist and ankles, but he didn't struggle. He knew, as I did, that he could not free himself quickly. And, of course, before he could try, he would have had to release my arm. He relaxed his hold on me but didn't free me. "So what are you up to?"

"Games. Farewell games."

"Your farewell or mine?"

"Mine. I'll take the bus in the morning. I wanted you to remember me fondly . . . to see what you'll be missing."

"Playful bondage? I don't believe you. Not our Jillian."

"You once said I liked to be in control sexually."

"So I did, and this *is* control. But you're not to be trusted."

"You've been unconscious for the last fifteen minutes. If I'd wanted to harm you, I could have done it easily. I could have gotten a knife."

David looked at me skeptically but with interest. I crossed my legs and with my free hand pushed open my robe and pulled up Mrs. Ellis's tunic, revealing black nylon stockings, a black garter belt, and white lace panties. "I thought you might like to watch me take these things off."

"That wouldn't be without interest."

"It's more interesting when you're vulnerable."

"Vulnerable to what?"

"To my whims."

"I'm really not the submissive type, Jillian."

"Aren't you, Ava? Little Ava."

David relaxed his grasp again, this time almost freeing me. The adrenaline that was released in his system when he woke up was thinning out. His alcoholic muddle was reasserting itself. I pulled free of him and stood up. I untied my robe and let it slip to the floor. David looked at me intently.

"Angelic," he said.

"But not a guardian angel," I said.

"A dark angel, perhaps?"

"Perhaps."

"That's the kind I like."

I lifted the tunic over my head and dropped it next to the robe. Then I sat down on the bed again.

"Ava," I said. "Sweet Ava."

I took David's free hand and tied it quickly to the bed. Then I placed my index fingers on either side of his throat at the carotid arteries and pressed with firmness, but not alarming force. David became unconscious in seconds and died within a minute.

I put my tunic on and went to Elizabeth's room. I kissed her cold hand. Then I returned to my room and began to pack.

33 | *A Suitable Life*

Neither Father nor I slept that night. We sat in the silent house and considered the future.

"I guess you don't have to be a companion anymore," Father said.

"No."

"That was getting too much attention, anyway."

"What's next, then?"

"I'm going to Chicago."

I smiled. There was a Count Basie–Jimmy Rushing blues that started with the words, "Going to Chicago; sorry that I can't take you."

"Can you take me?" I asked.

"I'm inviting you, but I'm not sure you'd find a suitable life there. Maybe you're a small-town person now. But you ought to try the city for a while. People are going to be looking for us. They'll look in small towns."

"Yes. I'll go with you. I'll get you settled, anyway."

I wondered if Father was right and that I would have a difficult time making a new life.

"My life has been based on illusions," I said.

"Like everyone else's life."

"David's, for example."

"And anyone else you can name. It's nothing to worry about. What we have to worry about is that we know we're going to Chicago, but not how we'll get there. The bus?"

"How do we get to the bus?"

"We could ask somebody to drive us. Charlie Blake, maybe. He might take us to Chicago. And we could tell him what happened. Somebody ought to know."

"Eva ought to be told."

"You can write her a letter. Or you can call her from Chicago."

Father was thinking more clearly than I was. "You arrange things," I said.

"You'll have to get me Charlie Blake. He told me he's playing at Walter's tonight."

Father talked to Charlie and—with me acting as his eyes—did the other things that had to be done.

When Charlie finished the last set at Walter's, he picked us up in front of the Dobb house. A standard part of our luggage was a small overnight case we called the nest-egg bag. It now held the gold and other jewelry that had been in Elizabeth's wall safe.

When our baggage was loaded in the car, Father asked me to guide him back into the house. We went first to a closet where kerosene for the lamps was stored. Father told me to take two of the cans. Then we went to Elizabeth's room. "Soak the rug with the kerosene," Father said.

"Do we have to do this? This eccentric old house. And beautiful Elizabeth."

"She's not beautiful now. And there'll be fewer questions this way. Besides, fire is purifying."

I wasn't convinced it was necessary, but I saturated the rugs in Elizabeth's room and then in David's. I threw lighted matches into each room, and we went quickly to the car.

When we were outside of town, I had Charlie pull the car off the road. The night was exceptionally dark, and the rapidly brightening glow on the horizon was clearly visible through the car's back window.

"Wow," Charlie said.

Father said, "What's it like?"

"It's like a flower blossoming," I said.

I thought of Elizabeth at the center of the blossom. I remembered her children's story about the phoenix, and I heard her voice speaking of the perfect summer. I heard her speak of the singular phoenix ascending, finding its heaven, being celebrated. Through my tears, I watched the flames change to a massive yellow pillar. At the top of the pillar was a fluttering of whiteness—a feathery fluttering that rose birdlike through a billow of smoke and into the peaceful darkness of the night sky.

The faint sound of a siren emerged from the silence, and Charlie started the engine and spun our wheels in the roadside gravel. I had thought the siren was behind us, but headlights and a red flasher suddenly appeared ahead of us.

Charlie stepped on the accelerator for a moment, but then eased off and touched the brake. "Oh shit," he said. "What do I do?"

"What's going on?" Father asked. He was out of his element. We all were. The car ahead of us had braked hard and pulled broadside across the road. It was a police car.

"Slow down, Charlie," I said. "Stop when you get to the police car. And let me out. Don't say anything at all, either of you."

As I had hoped, the person in the police car was Jay Barnett. We walked toward each other at the side of the road, out of the harshness of the vehicles' lights.

"There was an accident at the house," I said.

"So I see," Jay said, looking off to the distant flames. "Anyone who didn't get out of there?"

"Mrs. Dobb and her son, David."

"You're sure they didn't slip out at the last moment?"

"They couldn't have done that."

"People are going to wonder about you and your father. They're going to ask me about that."

220

"Let's discuss it," I said.

We got into the police car, and Jay turned the lights off and parked at the side of the road. Charlie did the same.

I thought of the first time I had met Jay. I remembered that he liked secrets and that he and I were alike. When we were parked, Jay took his hat off. He wants me to admire him, I thought. I wanted to kiss him, but I was afraid he might misinterpret the gesture and look on it as a little bribe. He said, "So what do I tell people?"

"Tell them it was murder and arson."

"What do I tell them about you?"

"Tell them I'm elusive."

"What happened, Jillian?"

"David killed his mother. I killed him."

"Nobody will grieve about Ms. David. Or about Elizabeth, either, I suspect. But they'll want the loss of that house avenged. Why the burning?"

I wasn't sure. Had Father just wanted to cover our tracks or to bring about some kind of purification? And suddenly I didn't care. For the first time, it occurred to me that I could simply surrender. My mission, if that's what it was, had been completed. I was just running to save Father. In a sense, everything had been for him. And I did not regret it. He used life well, in a way that I never could. I lived through him. But he could live without me.

I began to feel exhausted. I put my hand on Jay's hand. I noticed that I had let my nails grow longer than usual—my hands had become less practical, more decorative. "Jay," I said. "Let my father go. You can have me."

"I've already had you, Jillian."

I was about to say, "Then *they* can have me; *anyone* can have me," when I realized how weak I had become in the last few hours. Although my life would be less significant in the future, I need not be abject. I could still take pride in what I had accomplished. And there was a chance I might be needed once again.

I said to Jay, "The way I remember it, you didn't have me; I had you."

I was wearing a heavy wool skirt over knee-high socks. Jay raised the skirt and leaned down and lightly kissed each bare thigh. Then, less lightly, he kissed my mouth. "You've had me again," he said. "Go."

I ran back to Charlie's car and got in next to him. "You'd better go now," I said.

Charlie and Father pointed out, simultaneously, that Billie Holiday had written a song with that title.

Songs were their world. My world was the now-fading orange glow on the horizon and the flashing red lights that were receding behind us.

When we reached the suburbs of Chicago, I telephoned Eva and told her what had happened before the fire. She said nothing at first. When I asked her if she understood, she said, "I don't understand, but I heard what you said."

"I hope you don't blame me," I said. Eva hung up.

Charlie dropped Father and me off at a run-down hotel, and we began a new life. It began with sleep.

For a few weeks, stories about Father and me were on the television screens and in the newspapers. No one was sure what had happened to Elizabeth and David that night, but Father and I were blamed for starting the fire. Reporters traced us to other houses and other deaths, and we became another imperfectly understood legend of American terror.

Eventually, Father announced that his atonement was complete. He became the house pianist in a South Side lounge, and I took up a modest version of the "lush life" that Billy Strayhorn had described in his song.

I sleep in the day, and at night there is music and whiskey and the people who sit alone, those whom I occasionally offer casual and harmless companionship.

I see the world reflected through the mirror behind the bar. It was in that mirror that I looked up one day to see John Ellis, who was still enough of a detective to find us (he had called the musician's union) and who now umpires in the National League. He drops in when he's in town for a Cubs series.

John and Eva weren't together long. She travels through the Midwest buying, restoring, and reselling old houses, which she lives in during the restoration. She has never forgiven me for the burning of the Dobb house.

Shirley lives with Charlie Blake and is looking for a career that doesn't require much studying.

On the wall of the apartment I share with Father hangs the sketch of Elizabeth—the sketch Eva made during their summer of happiness. Occasionally, Father asks me to describe the portrait to him.

I often think of Officer Jay Barnett with more than one kind of gratitude, but I know I will never see him again.

I reread *Jane Eyre* occasionally. There is always a bookmark—a torn photograph of seven women—at the page on which Jane says of her blind husband what I can now say of Father: "All my confidence is bestowed on him, all his confidence is devoted to me; we are precisely suited in character—perfect concord is the result."

My life is a suitable life, I think, for a person whose soul is ransomed, for one who someday will be without her Father, one who might then resume an earlier way of life, who might stand once more at the stranger's door and say, "I understand you're looking for a companion."

Printed in the United States
By Bookmasters